Books by Dave Lowe

The Incredible Dadventure
A Mumbelievable Challenge
The Spectacular Holly-Day

The Stinky and Jinks series:
My Hamster Is a Genius
My Hamster Is an Astronaut
My Hamster Is a Spy
My Hamster's Got Talent
My Hamster Is a Pirate
My Hamster Is a Detective

Squirrel Boy Vs The Bogeyn
Squirrel Boy Vs The Squirrel H

THE MUMBELIEVABLE CHALLENGE

BY
DAVE
LOWE

Illustrated by The Boy Fitz Hammond

Piccadilly
PRESS

First published in Great Britain in 2017 by
PICCADILLY PRESS
80–81 Wimpole St, London W1G 9RE
www.piccadillypress.co.uk

Text copyright © Dave Lowe, 2017
Illustrations copyright © The Boy Fitz Hammond, 2017

A CIP catalogue record for this book is available from the British Library.

ISBN: 978-1-84812-589-6
also available as an ebook

1

Printed and bound by Clays Ltd, St Ives Plc

Piccadilly Press is an imprint of Bonnier Zaffre Ltd,
a Bonnier Publishing company
www.bonnierpublishing.com

For Stace, Bec and Miri: thanks for the best adventure ever.

*And for the incredible students and teachers
of the Shorncliffe State School Writers' Collective.*

1   The Challenge

It all started when Mum exploded.

Not literally. I mean, she didn't actually blow up or anything.

She just lost her temper. And for a lot of mums that might be a normal thing, but my mum is usually incredibly patient. She says – quite a lot – that she *has* to be patient, living with us.

The night in question was a school night, and we were all in the living room. Oates, our dog, was sprawled on the floor, exhausted from a long day of trying to scratch, sniff or lick pretty much everything in the entire world.

Dad was in his usual armchair, hunched over his laptop and tapping away at the keyboard.

Ernest, my almost two-year-old brother, was sitting on the floor, staring at the telly like he was in some kind of a trance. It was his favourite show, about a family of elephants who for some reason lived in a house and all walked on two legs, which is actually pretty weird, when you think about it. But Ernest was completely transfixed, as if he'd been hypnotised by all the swinging trunks.

I was on the sofa next to Mum. I was playing a game on her phone – an app called Jumping Guy. It was pretty addictive, and was about this guy that jumped a lot, but I guess you could probably have worked that out from the name.

So there we were, all of us happily doing our own thing – except Mum, who was doing a fair bit of sighing and tutting which, to be honest, made it pretty hard to concentrate on Jumping Guy.

Then suddenly it was *Mum* who was jumping up. She leapt out of her seat and shouted, 'Enough!'

Dad looked up from his computer screen, Ernest turned away from the telly, and even Oates pricked up his ears and lifted his head. I looked up from the phone for a moment and, when I looked back, Jumping Guy had plummeted to his death.

'You killed Jumping Guy,' I said to Mum.

'May he rest in peace,' she replied, and sighed. 'Here we are, together as a family, but look – you're all completely lost in your own little worlds. In Ernest's case, it's a world where elephants wear trousers, for heaven's sake. Dad's on the internet and you, Holly, are playing a game on the phone!'

3

'I'm actually working,' said Dad. 'Writing an email to my editor. She took all my commas out again.'

I like to tell people that my dad is an explorer, but according to Mum, he's actually a 'travel writer'. Either way, he has the coolest job in the entire world (apart from Harrison Duffy's mum, who works in an actual sweet shop and brings him home little bags of cola fizzes and flying saucers).

Mum was looking at me, as if to say, *Well, you certainly weren't working, Holly.*

'I was playing an educational game,' I explained.

'You were playing Jumping Guy.'

'Which is educational,' I said.

'How?'

'It warns about the dangers of jumping.'

'It's true,' said Dad. 'Jumping rarely ends well.'

And that's when Mum went a bit crazy.

She pounced like a ninja – a technology-hating ninja. She snatched the phone out of my hand, darted across to Dad and snapped his laptop shut. And, in one athletic sweeping movement, she spun around, lunged for the remote and clicked off the TV.

We all stared at her, open-mouthed, like you might stare at a monkey that had suddenly started breakdancing. It was surprising and funny – but also a little bit frightening.

'Now,' she said, gesturing to all of us, 'talk.'

Ernest started wailing because his show had been turned off, and Oates started woofing because Ernest was upset. Then Dad said, loudly, above all the noise, 'Nice weather we've been having, Holly!'

'What?!' I screeched, pretending not to hear him.

Mum – very loudly – groaned.

But that wasn't the end of it. In fact, it was only the start.

The next day at breakfast, Mum put down her bit of toast and looked at me and Dad with a serious expression.

'It's the Easter holidays in two weeks.'

She didn't need to tell *me* that. I'd been counting down ever since half-term.

'And,' she continued, 'I've come up with a challenge for the pair of you. You seem to think of yourselves as "adventurers" . . .'

'We certainly do,' said Dad. 'Don't we, Holly?'

I nodded.

'Then this,' she said, 'will be a piece of cake for you. Your challenge is to survive for five whole days without screens.'

'Easy,' said Dad. 'Easy-peasy, lemon squeezy.'

But I wasn't quite so sure, and I became even less sure when Mum added, 'Without electricity, in fact.'

'No electricity?' I said. 'But that's pretty much everything.'

Then Mum smiled and said, 'You'll be living in the wild,' and suddenly I was incredibly excited. I think I actually squealed.

'Just me and Dad?' I asked.

'And Oates,' Mum added. 'I've found a small cabin for you, in the woods.'

Dad was frowning mischievously. 'Sounds like a fairy tale,' he said. 'Have you checked that it doesn't belong to three bears? Or a wolf dressed up as a granny?'

I couldn't resist joining in. 'Is the cabin made of gingerbread?'

'Wood,' said Mum wearily. 'It's made of wood.'

'Ah,' said Dad. 'So it must belong to the second little pig then.'

Mum gave Dad a look. She normally enjoyed daft discussions – in fact, she usually liked to join in – but this was a look that said, *Can't we ever have normal conversations, like regular families?*

Dad took the hint.

'So,' he said, 'this cabin – where did you find it?'

'On the internet,' said Mum.

I thought about pointing out how funny it was that Mum had booked our 'screen-free' break *on the internet*. But she didn't look in the mood to laugh, so I kept quiet.

'It's in Fir Forest,' she said.

I knew Fir Forest. We'd been there for a walk once, before Ernest was born. It was an hour's drive away, not far from the safari park, and it seemed like the perfect place for a real adventure.

'The cabin belongs to an elderly couple,' she said, 'and they don't use it any more. The walk through the woods to get there is too much for them these days.'

'How far is it?' I asked nervously. I'd got blisters climbing Harold's Peak on my Dadventure last year, and that had only been a short distance.

'It's just a few kilometres,' she said. 'Nothing to trouble a fit ten-year-old girl and an energetic dog.' Then she looked at Dad with a jokey frown. 'And it should even be okay for a fairly out-of-condition middle-aged man,' she added.

'Hey,' said Dad, 'who are you calling middle-aged?'

But he was actually grinning too. 'It might make a great magazine piece – "A Dad, a Daughter and a Dog in the Wild".'

He looked really pleased with himself.

'So, Holly,' said Mum, 'what do you think?'

I was really excited – finally a proper adventure away from home, with Dad! 'Brilliant!' I replied, beaming at her. But then I thought of something, pulled a face and held my nose in mock-disgust. 'Five days though, in a small cabin, with Oates? He might get really stinky, don't you think?'

'After five days with no running water,' Mum said, 'the dog's probably going to smell much nicer than your father.'

2   Holiday Disasters

The last week of school before the holidays is normally brilliant.

The teachers stop doing spelling tests and times tables and instead do lots of fun stuff – sometimes we even get to watch a movie, with popcorn.

So, when I walked into class on the Monday morning, I was in a happy mood – looking forward to a fun week at school, followed by what my Mum was calling 'The Screen-Free Wildlife Adventure', and what Dad was calling 'The Mumbelievable Challenge', because, a) it was Mum's idea and, b) Dad loves terrible puns.

As soon as I walked into class though, I noticed the giggles.

I often get this feeling that people are laughing at me, but usually it turns out that they are laughing at something else completely.

Since my performance in the school talent show, and since I'd made a few good friends at school, I hardly ever got teased any more. But this time kids really did seem to be looking at me, then looking at each other, and then sniggering. I was sure I wasn't imagining it. I checked the buttons on my shirt to make sure I hadn't missed one. I checked that I hadn't tucked my skirt into my knickers. I rubbed my face with the back of a hand to make sure there wasn't any breakfast still on there.

But the laughter – giggling, sniggering – continued.

My skin was feeling incredibly hot.

Then Emily Fellows said something to me – in a loud whisper so that everyone (except Ms Devenport, our teacher) could hear: 'Well done for wearing clothes today, Holly.'

There was more laughter – a lot more. I had no idea what she was talking about. But I had that horrible prickly feeling – the one you get when everyone except you is in on the joke.

I sat down next to Asha Chopra, who was my best friend. She wasn't joining in at least, but she *was* looking really embarrassed for me.

'What?' I whispered.

'You were in the weekend newspaper,' she whispered back, but I still didn't have any idea what she was talking about.

'Me? Holly Chambers?' I said, like I needed to make it clear which 'me' I was talking about.

'It was something your dad wrote,' she explained. 'It was called "Holiday Disasters". Mum showed me. It completely cracked her up – she actually snorted her coffee out of her nose.'

I frowned.

'You were staying in a posh hotel with your mum and dad, a few years ago. You'd stripped off to go to the bathroom for a shower, but you took the wrong door and walked right out of your hotel room instead. The door clicked shut behind you, and you were –' she whispered the next bit – 'completely naked, in the hotel corridor.'

I could hardly breathe.

I'd only been five years old, but I remembered it really clearly. Doing an accidental nudie-run in a fancy hotel isn't something that you easily forget.

I'd banged on the door to get back in, but my parents couldn't hear me over the sound of the movie they were watching on the TV. Then I heard a family coming down the corridor, and I freaked out and ran away – hid in the corridor, behind a big vase. But when they'd gone, I had this even more horrible realisation – I didn't know the number of our room, and all of the doors looked exactly the same. Luckily, after a few minutes, a cleaner found me and wrapped me up in a dressing gown and took me to reception. The manager called Mum and Dad, who were still sitting on the bed watching the movie – they hadn't even noticed that I was missing.

It was one of those stories that often got told at family gatherings. Like the story about when Mum milked a cow and it pooed all over her shoes, or the time that Dad got lost in a rainforest and had to be rescued by the Brazilian army.

Dad telling the hotel story to my grandparents or family friends at a barbecue – that was one thing. But putting it in the newspaper, for the entire country to read – that was different. That was wrong. Completely humiliating.

And he must have known that it would be embarrassing for me, because he always showed me any articles of his that were in the newspaper and this time he hadn't.

I felt sick, betrayed.

I whispered urgently to Asha, 'Did the story mention me running naked down the corridor?'

'Yes.'

I sighed.

'Hiding behind a vase?'

She nodded.

'Being found by a cleaning lady?'

Asha nodded again, and she must have seen the look on my face.

'Look, not everyone gets a newspaper, do they?' she said kindly. 'And there are loads of different papers too. Plus, most kids in this class would never read one anyway. Harrison only reads joke books and comics. The Harmer twins only read books about ballerinas or fairies, or fairies who are also ballerinas. Emily is probably too busy checking herself out in the mirror to read *anything*.'

At that moment, Emily Fellows reached into her schoolbag and pulled out the newspaper cutting. She did it with a real flourish, like she was pulling a rabbit from a top hat. It was a full-page article, with 'Holiday Disasters' in big letters, and a cartoon of a naked girl – *me*! – accompanying it.

'That's Holly!' said a boy. There was a huge peal of laughter.

'Holly's a streaker!' said someone else.

I bowed my head. I bit my lip – otherwise I would definitely have burst into hot, uncontrollable tears.

* * *

When I got home from school, I went straight to my room, threw myself on the bed, buried my head in my pillow and cried. Except that 'cried' doesn't really do it justice. It was more like loud sobbing, mixed with random wails, squeaks and hiccups. I made some noises I hadn't known I was capable of.

I hadn't cried so much since the time I'd let go of my red kite in the park when I was little and I'd watched it sail away until it was a tiny red speck among the clouds. But this was even worse, because you can always buy a new kite. You can't erase the memories of an entire school.

Mum came into my room, followed by Ernest and Oates. In my family you can never be alone for more than a few minutes.

Ernest was saying, 'Olly ky-ing,' over and over, which means 'Holly's crying' in Ernest-lish. Oates was licking my legs with his tongue – it felt like damp, drooly sandpaper. Neither my brother nor the dog were making me feel any better.

'What's up, Sausage?' Mum asked gently. 'Bad day at school, was it?'

18

I nodded. I'd stopped crying now, but my cheeks were still itchy from all the tears.

'Tell me all about it,' she said, sitting down on the bed next to me.

For the longest time, I didn't say anything. And then I said, 'Dad's completely ruined my life.'

'Welcome to the club,' she said, before quickly adding, 'Joke.'

But I wasn't laughing. Dad *had* ruined my life. I told her all about it, and I'd been worried that she was going to tell me I was just being silly, that I was over-reacting. But when I'd finished she just hugged me, kissed the top of my head and said, 'Oh, you poor little sausage.'

Six days later, the night before Dad and I were due to go on our adventure, I was sitting on my bed again. I wasn't crying this time, but I was in a pretty bad mood. Dad had taken Ernest and Oates for a walk to the duck pond, but I hadn't wanted to join them.

Mum poked her head in.

'You've not started packing yet?'

I shook my head.

'I don't want to go,' I said, so she came in and sat beside me.

'I thought you'd be really excited. You always said that you wanted to go on an adventure with Dad. And here it is – an actual real-life adventure.' When I shrugged, she added, 'You're still pretty angry with him, aren't you?'

I nodded. I was still furious. He'd apologised – a lot – but I'd been the one who'd spent the entire last week of school getting teased. Pretty much the whole school had seen that cartoon of my naked bum and heard the whole embarrassing story, thanks to Emily Fellows.

She was going to Disneyland for *her* holiday. She'd been bragging about it for months, and talked about all the rides she'd be going on: Pirates of the Caribbean, Splash Mountain, the Haunted Mansion. Me, I was going to be spending five days in a log cabin with the man who'd made me a complete laughing stock.

'Dad's still really looking forward to going though,' said Mum.

'He's probably hoping I fall over, or get attacked by a wolf, so he can write a hilarious story about it.'

Mum chuckled. 'Well, the good news is, there aren't

any wolves in those woods. No big bad ones. And not even any small nice ones. No dangerous animals, in fact, of any kind.'

'He must be hoping I get savaged by a rabbit then.'

'Well, you'd have to admit, a surprise bunny attack *would* make a pretty good story.' Mum smiled kindly. 'Look – tell you what – you lay out the stuff that you want to take, and I'll pack it for you. How's that sound?'

I sighed. Then nodded.

Mum is a world-class packer. I'm more of a throw-everything-into-a-suitcase kind of person, and then I'm a jump-up-and-down-on-the-suitcase-until-the-lid-will-close kind of person. Mum stuffs socks into shoes, rolls T-shirts up into little balls and somehow manages to fit everything in. It's like that magic bag in *Mary Poppins* with the lamp and furniture tucked away inside!

When she came back into my room a few minutes later, she looked at what I'd laid out on my bed and raised her eyebrows.

'You're only going away for five days, Holly,' she said. 'Not for the rest of your life.'

'But these are just the absolute essentials.'

She burst out laughing.

'When you're packing for an expedition, you really need to work out what is a "need", Holly, and what is a "want". For example, *one* teddy bear isn't essential, let alone *five*. Two full pencil cases?'

'One's for crayons, the other for felt-tips,' I said, as if it was completely obvious.

'Six books? Impossible. Choose one teddy, a couple of pens, one book.'

'One book? To last me a whole week without the telly or the internet?'

'Books are really heavy, love, and the cabin's a two-hour walk from where I'm dropping you off.'

'So let me take Dad's iPad. I can put loads of books on there – and it's really light.'

'What part of "no screens" don't you understand?'

'The "no" part?'

'Funny,' Mum said. 'Anyway, where would you even plug it in? Into a tree? And you're there with Dad. He's a writer – get *him* to tell you stories.'

I groaned. But Mum smiled again and fished something out of her jeans pocket. It was an old-fashioned pocket watch, silver and round, and it fitted snugly inside her hand. She passed it to me. It had a satisfying weight to it and it looked like something from an antiques show on the telly. There was an extra dial on top too, the size of a small coin.

'Take this with you,' Mum said. 'It was my grandma's. She enjoyed quite a few adventures herself, back in the days when women weren't really meant to do those kinds

of things. It's beautiful, isn't it? And not all technology needs electricity, you see? You just need to wind the little button on the side, once a day. And that thing on top is actually a compass, to tell you which direction is north. Dad will be able to show you how to use it. Now – let's finish packing, shall we?'

3 A Walk in the Woods

Mum had been right: I was glad I'd packed light. According to my pocket watch, it had only been fifty-two minutes since Mum and Ernest had dropped us off in the car park. So we weren't even halfway there yet – but my back was already aching from the weight of my bag.

Dad's rucksack was more than twice as big – with both of our blankets and pillows rolled up on top, it was almost as big as he was. It was a miracle that the weight of it hadn't toppled him backwards and, if it did, I wasn't sure that he'd be able to get back up onto his feet – I imagined him stuck there like an upside-down tortoise, kicking his legs helplessly and waggling his head. But though he'd stumbled a few times – we both had – he'd so far managed to stay upright.

The journey through the woods was much harder than I'd expected. No wonder the old couple who owned the cabin couldn't manage the journey any more. I'd thought there would be a path, like there always was in fairy tales. And there was a kind of track, some of the way. But we also had to weave between trees, stumble over rocks and climb over roots. Oates was much better at this than I was – but then again, he had twice as many legs as me, and no backpack. He seemed to be having the best time ever – hundreds of new things to sniff, and thousands of new creatures to bark at. Plus, millions of trees to wee against. This was like a theme park for him.

Dad stopped suddenly and glanced around, scratching his head.

'What?' I panted.

'Just getting my bearings,' he said.

'What's that supposed to mean?'

'It means, I'm just trying to work out where we are.'

'So we're lost?'

'Not at all,' he said. But then he rubbed his chin and kept looking around. 'It's just that one tree looks pretty much like another, don't you think?'

I grunted. For an explorer, Dad had a terrible sense of direction.

He reached into his pocket and pulled out a map – the one he'd printed off from the internet – unfolded it and traced our journey with a finger.

'I think we're around here,' he said, tapping the map and showing it to me. 'That blue line over there is a stream. And that brown dot there is the cabin.'

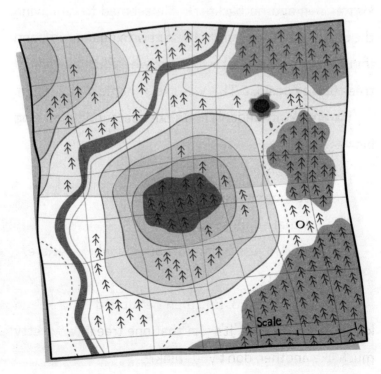

'What's the red dot?' I asked.

'Jam, I think,' he said. He'd been planning the route over breakfast, and now he wiped the red dot off with a finger and tasted it. 'Strawberry.'

'Yuck.'

He grinned and pulled a compass out of his pocket. 'Let me teach you how to use this thing, Lolly.'

'It's Holly,' I said, because I didn't want him to think I'd forgiven him.

Dad demonstrated how to find north on the compass, and held out the map, saying, 'So, where's the cabin?'

I took a guess.

He shook his head. 'This is north,' he said, pointing.

'And here's the cabin on the map. So – which way?'

I pointed again.

'I think you're right,' he said.

'"Think"?'

'If we knew exactly where we were going, and exactly how to get there,' he said, 'it would hardly be an adventure, would it?'

I sighed. Here I was, lost in the woods with Dad – who'd humiliated me in front of the whole country – and with Oates, whose life's ambition was to wee on absolutely everything in the entire world.

Dad started walking again. So did Oates. I had to struggle to keep up.

In the next hour, we stopped three more times – to drink some water from Dad's bottle, and so that he could consult the map again, shake his head, check the compass and rub his chin a lot.

It wasn't just my back that was killing me – by now my whole body was aching. This was beginning to feel like the worst holiday ever, and we hadn't even arrived yet.

The third time we stopped, I snapped.

'We're completely lost, aren't we?'

'Not lost exactly – more . . . misplaced. A bit. The cabin really should be around here,' he said, as if someone might have moved it.

That's when I glimpsed a wooden building through the trees.

'There!' I said.

Dad squinted, then thrust his arms in the air, like a footballer who'd just scored a goal.

'Woohoo! Well spotted, Lolly!'

'*Holly.*'

'Sorry!'

The cabin was on a flattish, treeless area of dirt the

size of a tennis court. As we got closer though, it looked less like a log cabin and more like an old hut – a hut that no one had been in for ages. It had looked a lot bigger in the photo we'd seen on the website. A lot newer too.

The door was padlocked shut. Dad had the key, but the padlock was rusty, and it took a long time – and loads of muttering – before he could force the door open. It was stiff and creaky, like a door in a scary movie. Oates darted in and we followed him. Dad shrugged off his backpack, and so did I. It was an amazing feeling – so incredibly light. My shoulders felt free, relaxed.

I glanced around, and the amazing feeling slipped away.

There were bunk beds. A small square wooden table and two chairs. A small fireplace, with a shovel, an axe and a poker leaning against it. A black pot, hanging. Cobwebs everywhere. A thin layer of dust.

And that was pretty much it. Not much to see. But there was a fair bit to smell.

'Looks very cosy,' said Dad.

I rolled my eyes.

'"Cosy" would not be the word that I'd use.'

'Oh? What about "homely" then? Or "rustic"?'

I shook my head.

'"Quaint"?' he suggested.

'It stinks, Dad.'

Dad sniffed theatrically.

'There is a faint whiff of something,' he admitted. 'We'll leave the door open and let some fresh air in. It'll come good.'

It didn't take Oates long to find out where the smell was coming from. He was barking at a dead rat, in the corner by the fireplace. I pulled a face. Emily Fellows, at this very moment, would probably be on a roller coaster, or high-fiving with Mickey and Minnie Mouse.

Me, I was in the middle of nowhere, sharing a shed with my dad, the dog and a dead rodent.

4 The Cabin

Dad picked up the shovel, scooped up the dead rat, walked outside and hurled it as far he could. Then he came back inside and said, 'Now, who's feeling peckish?'

Oates barked. Nothing put *him* off his food.

Dad unzipped his rucksack and pulled out Oates's bowl and the packet of dry dog food.

I sat at the table and opened my bag. I took out my book, and was about to unpack my clothes when I saw something unfamiliar in there: a big brown envelope, with my name on the front in Mum's handwriting.

I tore it open, and inside were five smaller envelopes, each one a different colour. I tipped them out onto the table. On each was written a day of the week. Some of the envelopes were fat, like they had some kind of object inside, and some looked like they just contained a letter.

And folded up, not inside an envelope, was this note:

Hi Holly,

You didn't think that the challenge would be a piece of cake, did you? I mean, surviving without screens won't be easy and you'll have to put up with Oates's bottom and Dad's terrible jokes for five whole days. But I wanted to make it even more challenging for you, Holly (and even more fun)!

So, there's a task for every day, including today, and there'll be a prize if you complete them all.

Good luck!

Can't wait to see you again.

Lots of love,

Mum x

I ripped open the yellow envelope which had 'Monday' on the front, and two small chocolate bars fell out.

Today's Task:
Build a fire and
cook dinner on it.
(Here's your pudding.)

CHOCO!

CHOCO!

Dad read it, grinned, then reached into his rucksack and pulled out a small, thick book called *The Survival Manual*. He opened it to a page with an illustration of a fire and put it on the table in front of me.

Building a fire was actually a really good idea right now.

For the first few minutes after we arrived, I was still warm and a bit sweaty from all the walking, but then I cooled down and realised that the cabin was pretty cold – colder than outside. So I went out to collect lots of wood: small sticks for kindling and fallen branches to put on top. Oates came to help too, if, by 'help', you mean 'weeing on random trees'.

Once I had an armful of sticks, we came back inside. Dad had dusted and got rid of the cobwebs. I built a fire, using the scrunched-up yellow envelope from today's task as the tinder, and a small pyramid of sticks. It took three matches to get it going, and then I used my book to fan the tiny flames. Within minutes, unbelievably, I had a proper fire going. Dad gave me a little nod of approval. I had a really warm glow, and not just from the fire: I felt like an actual adventurer.

In the afternoon, I was sitting on the bottom bunk reading my book. It was about this shy boy who lived in an orphanage and was bullied – but who had found a portal to another world, a world which he had to save. It was the second in the series, and it was really good. Dad was at the table, unpacking some of the things from his backpack and lining them up – candles, two metal cups, two plastic dishes, two towels, a toilet roll . . .

'Where's the toilet?' I asked because, thinking about it, I'd walked right around the cabin when I was collecting the firewood and hadn't seen one.

'We're in the woods,' Dad said. 'The wild.'

'And?'

'Everywhere's the loo,' he said. 'Mice don't use tiny mouse toilets, do they?'

'But I'm not a mouse,' I pointed out.

'You're an expert in animal poo though,' he said, which was actually true. (I'll explain later.) 'Where do you think the animals all go?'

I must have looked completely horrified, because he grinned and said, 'Don't worry, there's a treasure box around the back. Pure luxury.'

I frowned again, so he took me outside to see it.

The treasure box was not nearly as lovely as it sounded. It was a wooden box, knee-height, with a lid that Dad removed to reveal a very deep round hole, and a completely horrible smell.

'That's the toilet,' he said. 'Do you need to go?'

I shook my head. I could wait. All week if necessary. All year.

But then, only an hour later, I just couldn't hold on any more. I'd drunk too much water on our walk. I couldn't face the treasure box yet though, so I followed Oates's example and did a wee behind a tree.

That evening I cooked canned tomato soup, bubbling in a pot which hung on the hook above the fire – my fire. We ate the soup in bowls at the table, mopping it up with wodges of bread. When Dad had finished, he pushed his bowl away and leant back in his chair.

'This is the life,' he said, unwrapping his chocolate from Mum. 'So peaceful, isn't it? So calm.'

I shrugged.

'What?' he said.

'It's *too* peaceful. It's a bit – boring.'

'Boring? With the two of us for company?'

He looked at Oates, who was under the table, snoring.

'There's nothing to do here, Dad. No telly, no internet. No Jumping Guy.'

'What do you think people did hundreds of years ago?' he asked. I shrugged again. 'I'll tell you what they did – they made their own entertainment. Singing songs, playing games, putting on shows.'

'If you're thinking of doing one of your puppet shows with a pair of socks,' I said, 'I'm definitely not in the mood.'

'You used to love my sock-puppets.'

'I also used to love eating baby food,' I said. 'And sucking my thumb, and playing Peepo!. People change,

Dad. They grow up. At least, most people do.'

He ignored this and pointed at the fire.

'Just take a look at that,' he said. 'It's just completely mesmerising, isn't it? I could watch it for hours. It never gets boring. So much better than the telly.'

I frowned at him, trying to work out if he was being serious or not.

He was being serious.

'But there's only one channel,' I said. '"The Fire Channel". And it's the same show every night.'

'Is it though?' he said, as if he wasn't talking about a small fire, but a wonder of the world. 'Just look at those colours. The reds, oranges, yellows. The tiniest hint of blue. The crackle, the dance of the flames. The warmth. It's proper reality TV, is that.'

I watched it for a bit, and I had to admit Dad was actually kind of right. Not that it was better than telly (although it was loads more interesting than those renovations shows Mum likes, where posh people build their own houses and everything always takes ages longer than they thought it was going to, and then the windows come and they're not the right size, and then it snows, and they're living in a caravan and arguing because they've already spent too much money).

But there is something very nice about a fire, especially one that you've built yourself. Something relaxing about it too. I felt my head nodding forward, my eyelids closing and my breathing slowing down.

The next time I opened my eyes, everything was covered in pale light: it was morning! And I was in the bottom bunk, tucked in.

5 Five Interesting Things

I opened Tuesday's envelope as soon as I got up. It was orange, and there was no chocolate inside this time, but there was a pencil, a folded-up sheet of blank paper and a note:

Hi, Holly,

Hope you had a good sleep.

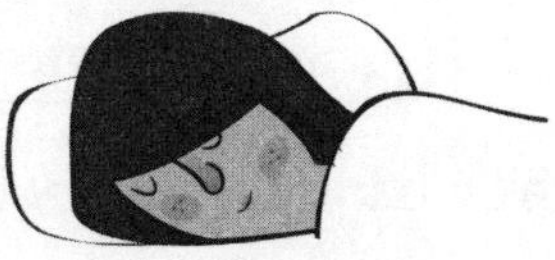

Today's task: explore!

Find 5 interesting things,

and draw them for me.

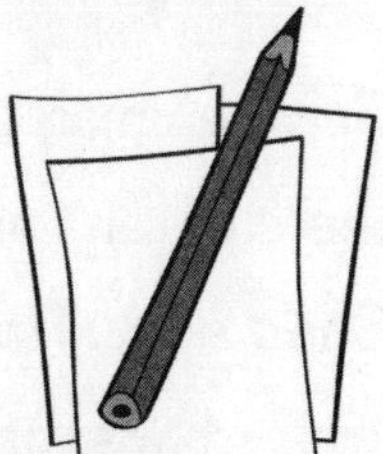

Have tons of fun!

Lots of love,

Mum

Dad read it over my shoulder.

'Well,' he said, 'you've already found me and Oates, so only three to go.'

'She said "interesting *things*", not "interesting smells".'

Dad laughed. Then he sniffed his armpits and pulled a face. 'I guess I could do with a bit of a wash.'

'Yes, you could. And not just a *bit* of one either.'

I wound up the pocket watch, like Mum had shown me, then Dad passed me a muesli bar and a handful of dried apricots.

'You'll need energy if you're going to go exploring. Take Oates with you for protection.'

'From what?'

Dad shrugged. 'If you come across any scary animals, he'll bark at them, won't he? Or at least he'll sniff their bottoms.'

'Scary animals?' I said, suddenly nervous. 'Mum told me there weren't any around here.'

'She's right. I'm joking. You might get nibbled by a squirrel – that's the worst that might happen. Tickled by a mouse. Pooped on by a bird. That kind of thing.'

I nodded, relieved, though I really hoped that I wouldn't be target practice for any birds.

'What are *you* going to do this morning?' I asked.

He leant back in his chair, spread his arms wide and a huge smile swept over his face.

'There's absolutely nothing to do,' he said, like that

was the best thing ever. 'I might read my book. Or collect some wood and put the telly on,' he said, nodding at the fireplace.

After 'breakfast', I went out into the woods, with the pencil and paper in my hand and Oates at my heels.

Straight away I saw lots of *quite* interesting things: delicate white flowers, little birds, dark berries, insects flitting around, but nothing that was *super*-interesting, and I really wanted to surprise Mum. Whenever we went out on nature walks (not so often these days, since Ernest came along), Mum would forever be pointing out beautiful things, with intricate patterns and shapes, so I was determined to find some for her.

Oates found the first one for me. He spotted a spectacular toadstool at the base of a tree. I'd never seen one like it before – not in real life at least. It was like a toadstool in a storybook: the size of my hand and red with white spots. I half expected an elf to leapfrog over it at any moment.

Oates was sniffing it, so I shooed him away, because it looked poisonous and he would probably be daft enough to give it a nibble.

When I'd finished sketching that, we walked deeper into the woods, and only a minute or two later I saw my second interesting thing – a spider's web. Now, you might not think that a web is super-interesting, but this one was completely perfect. It sparkled in the morning light, with drops of dew like tiny diamonds. It was much harder to draw than the toadstool, and it took me ages, so Oates got a bit impatient and wandered off. By the time I'd finished drawing the web, he was nowhere to be seen. But he wasn't hard to find, because he'd started barking really loudly: I guessed that he'd seen a fly.

Some dogs go crazy in thunderstorms. Others go nuts if they spot a cat or a squirrel. Oates is special. He gets completely freaked out by flies.

When I caught up to him, however, I saw that it wasn't a fly that had got him worked up this time, but a butterfly instead. A completely stunning one too. Deep blue, green and yellow, and it was resting on a branch just out of Oates's reach. I sketched it quickly before it flew off. I could add more details back at the cabin later.

Now that Oates had stopped barking, everything was peaceful again, and I kind of understood what Dad meant, about how nice it was to have nothing to do – to have nobody around, no distractions. Just nature.

I'd found three interesting things already, and I wandered around looking for number four, in no rush at all. A few things caught my eye as I explored – a heart-shaped leaf, a snail whose shell had a cool pattern, some bright green moss – but nothing that completely wowed me, so I kept going. And then I spotted something in the dirt:

Worm poo.

You might think that it's a bit weird, with plants and birds and wildlife everywhere, to choose a poo as one of my five interesting things . . . But this was no ordinary poo. It was no bigger than my thumb, but was made up of tiny squiggles of dirt, and the more I studied it, the more it looked like a magnificent sculpture, like something out of the modern-art gallery we went to with school.

Dad wasn't joking when he'd called me a 'poo expert' yesterday. We have this game called 'Plop Trumps' – he bought it for me – where every card has a photo of an animal dropping, complete with fascinating facts. Fascinating to me at least. Did you know that a goose

poos every twelve minutes? My dad seems to forever be on the toilet but, even compared to him, that's pretty impressive work.

Mum found it all slightly disgusting, and wouldn't let us play it at the dinner table. But Dad and I had played it so many times that I'd pretty much memorised each card.

So I crouched and sketched the worm casting (which

is the posh way of saying it) and I'd almost finished when Oates started barking again. I tried to ignore him – he must have spotted yet another flying insect. If he barked at every bug he met, he'd lose his voice before the end of the day, which might not be a completely terrible thing.

'Shush, boy,' I said, but he kept on barking. So I looked up.

Then I shrieked, and tumbled backwards into the dirt.

Standing there – only a metre away from us – was a boy.

6 Zeb

The boy looked down at me as I was sprawled on the ground. He was wearing a red cap, looked a bit older than me and had thick dark eyebrows and a serious expression.

When Oates finally stopped barking, the boy said, 'Hey. Who are *you*?'

'Who are *you*?' I asked.

'I'm Zeb,' he said, and held out a hand to help me up. I ignored it – I was hardly a damsel in distress – and got up by myself. Then I brushed myself off.

'I'm Holly,' I said – well, I practically squeaked it, because my heart was still racing.

'If you don't mind me asking,' he said, 'what *is* that

strange thing you were sketching just now?' He had a posh voice – he pronounced his *g*'s. I wondered if he might be making fun of me, but then he added, 'It looks really cool.'

'Worm poo,' I explained. And then, because 'worm poo' is never a good answer to any question, I said, 'Worms eat their own body weight every day.' I looked Zeb up and down. 'Which is like you eating a hundred cheeseburgers, every single day of your life.'

He smiled warmly. 'I could actually kill for a cheeseburger

right now. I wonder where the nearest fast-food place is.' He looked around, as if there might be a McDonald's hidden among the trees. 'What are you doing here anyway? Apart from drawing poo, I mean.'

He was definitely teasing me, but there was a twinkle in his eye – he was trying to be funny, not mean.

I still blushed though. I couldn't help it.

'I'm camping. With my dad. You?'

'Same,' he said. 'Where's your tent?'

'We're in a cabin,' I said, 'not far from here.' Then I looked around. I couldn't see it – I'd wandered further than I'd thought, and I wasn't even sure any more which direction the cabin was in. 'It's somewhere around here,' I said, trying not to seem flustered. 'What about you?'

'Our tent's just over there,' he said, pointing. 'My dad says that staying in a cabin isn't really camping.' Then he rolled his eyes, to show that he didn't agree with his dad on this. '"Too much luxury," he says.'

'He's obviously not seen *our* cabin then.'

'So where is it – this cabin?'

I glanced around, and then shrugged.

'Are you lost?' he asked.

'No – I'm just getting my bearings.' Then I had an idea: I bent down, patted Oates, and said, 'Home, boy.'

But instead of leading the way back to the cabin, like a dog in a movie would, Oates just padded over to Zeb and sniffed his trainers – expensive Nike ones. I sighed. Zeb smiled.

And then, to change the subject from the fact that I was almost certainly lost, and that Oates was possibly the most useless dog in history, I said, 'So, is it just you and your dad camping?'

'Yep. My sisters get to stay home with Mum, doing girl things.'

That annoyed me a bit. What were 'girl things' anyway? Skipping? Giggling? Making pom-poms? But then Zeb smiled at me and said, 'Cracking dog you've got,' and I instantly forgave him. 'What's his name?'

'Oates – with an e.'

I was preparing to explain – for the millionth time – why he had such an unusual name, when Zeb said, 'Oh, like the polar explorer?'

'Yes,' I said, unable to hide my surprise. I'd thought that it was only our dorky family that knew the names of explorers. 'And my brother's named Ernest after . . .'

'Ernest Shackleton?' he guessed. I nodded. 'So who are you named after, Holly?'

I shrugged. 'After an annoying spiky plant, I suppose.'

This made him smile. He ruffled Oates's fur. Oates licked his hand.

'He's very friendly,' Zeb said.

'Yeah – friendly, but not exactly a brainiac. He's my dad's dog really, and they say that dogs take after their owners, don't they?'

Zeb smiled.

'It must be the same with guinea pigs,' he said. 'My sisters have two – they look cute, but they bite and scratch and smell a bit. The guinea pigs too.'

I laughed, but stopped suddenly because there was a loud shout – a man's voice. Not my dad's. This was deeper, boomier.

'Ahoy!'

I jumped. Oates barked. A man was walking over. He was about the same age as my dad, but strong-looking. He wore a black bandana, a black vest and trousers with lots of pockets.

'Hello,' he said to me. 'What's your name, little girl?'

Little girl? I wanted to say. *LITTLE GIRL?!* But instead I just said, 'Holly.'

'Nice to meet you, Holly. I'm Hunter, Zeb's dad.' He had a posh voice too, like someone from an old movie. He shook my hand – it was a real bone-cruncher – and flashed a smile. His teeth were like something from a toothpaste advert, neat and sparkly. 'You're camping here too, I take it, Holly?'

'In a log cabin.'

'Ah,' said Hunter, as if he was disappointed by this information. 'Where?'

I shrugged.

'So you're lost, are you?'

I was about to protest, but I *was* actually a bit lost, so I didn't say anything.

'Well,' said Hunter, 'I know a fair bit about tracking – following trails, I mean. I've been trying to teach young Zeb here, and he's slowly getting the hang of it. So we can help you find your way back, if you like.'

I looked at Zeb, who seemed to deflate a bit – he blushed and looked at his feet.

Hunter crouched and studied the ground around me.

'I'm checking for footprints, broken sticks, things like that.' Then he nodded. 'This way,' he said with certainty, and we all followed him.

It wasn't long before we found the cabin. Dad was sitting on the front step, reading a book by Charles Dickens.

'Ahoy!' Hunter called, and Dad looked up at us, surprised, put the book down and then stood up.

'Hello!' Dad said.

Hunter bounded over to him and shook his hand – another bone-cruncher, judging by the look on Dad's face.

'I'm Jim,' Dad said. 'Nice to meet you. I see you've already met Holly.'

'Hunter Wright,' said the man. 'And this is my son, Zeb. Your daughter was a bit lost, I think.'

I blushed and shook my head.

'Lost? Or just misplaced?' Dad asked me, with a wink. He was trying to make me feel better, but it just embarrassed me even more. Then, to Hunter and Zeb, he said, 'She must get her sense of direction from me. I once got lost in a supermarket, believe it or not. Now, can I get you boys a drink?'

'We're good, thanks,' said Hunter. 'We've got some nettle tea brewing, back at the tent.'

'Tent, huh?'

Hunter smiled. 'We don't believe in cabins,' he said. 'We really like to get down with nature.'

Zeb looked as embarrassed by *his* dad as I was with mine – which is really saying something.

'We've been doing it every year since Zeb was seven, haven't we, son?'

Zeb nodded meekly.

'He's got two big sisters at home. So we come here, just the two of us, a bit of father–son bonding, you know – a family tradition. I used to do it with my dad,

back in the day. We try to survive the way cavemen did –
foraging for food, collecting our own water, fishing in the
stream, that kind of thing.'

I thought he might have been joking, but he actually
looked serious.

Dad looked down at their fancy trainers and said,
with a cheeky grin, 'Nice shoes, cavemen!'

I glared at Dad – he was so embarrassing. Hunter's
face dropped, but Zeb flashed me an awkward smile, like
he agreed and thought it was funny. 'Come on, Dad,' he
said. 'The nettle tea will be boiling.'

Hunter nodded, said goodbye, and marched off with
Zeb following behind him.

* * *

At lunchtime, Dad and I were sitting at the table, reading. 'Are you hungry?' he asked. 'I was planning on foraging a can of baked beans from my bag.'

I rolled my eyes – Dad thought he was completely hilarious – but then I nodded and he lit the fire and poured the beans into the pot. Oates was having a nap. I took a break from my book and looked at the piece of paper that I'd drawn my sketches on: the toadstool, the web, the butterfly and the worm poo. Four things: I'd still needed one more when Zeb had interrupted me. But now, instead of going back outside, I decided it would be pretty funny to draw Zeb, from memory. His eyebrows were really easy to do at least – like hairy little caterpillars.

Dad glanced over and saw what I was doing.

'So he's interesting, is he?'

I blushed, and shrugged my shoulders.

'He seemed like a nice kid,' Dad said.

'Yeah. He knows about explorers too. He knew who Captain Oates and Shackleton were.'

'Good man,' said Dad, impressed.

'But then when his Dad came along, he seemed a bit

different. His dad's one of those super-confident guys, isn't he? When he was there, Zeb seemed to . . . shrink.'

Dad nodded.

'It's not easy being a dad though, Holly. You don't get classes telling you what to do. But Hunter says "ahoy" instead of "hello", he wears a bandana and a muscle vest, and he named his son "Zeb"! Now, one of those things, you could probably get away with. But, all of them . . . ?'

'You're just jealous because he's got bigger muscles than you.'

'Has he?' said Dad. 'I didn't notice.' But then he couldn't keep a straight face. 'All right – maybe I did notice – a tiny bit.' He chuckled. 'But this is the only muscle that really counts,' he said, tapping the top of his head. 'Don't you forget that, Holly.'

'His brain's probably bigger than yours too,' I said.

'Hey!' Dad pretended to look upset. Then he smiled. 'You're probably right though.'

I was in a strange mood all afternoon. I felt restless, but I didn't really want to go exploring.

After a bit I went outside, hoping that Zeb might

come over, but he wasn't around. So I threw a stick for Oates. You'd think, with all the sticks lying around, that he wouldn't actually bother chasing one, but he did, again and again and again. It was the same thing with Ernest and Peepo! Babies never get tired of Peepo! and dogs never get bored of chasing. I wished that I could be more like that. But I get bored really easily these days.

Back inside, I played cards with Dad and we shared a packet of ginger-nut biscuits. After the fifth game (I was winning 4–1), I yawned – a big, open-mouthed, arms-stretched-above-my-head yawn.

'What is it?' Dad said. 'You're not getting tired of beating me, are you?'

'I'm just a bit bored.'

'Bored?' said Dad, in disbelief. 'Again? Here? With so much to do?'

'Like what? And don't say, "Watch the fire," again.'

That was what he'd been going to say, so now he glanced around the cabin.

'When I was a kid, I used to play with whatever was lying around. A branch from a tree, for example.'

'A branch.'

'Yes . . .' he said, unconvincingly.

'What did you do? Whack Uncle Phil with it?'

'Yes,' he said, grinning. 'No. Look – it wasn't *that* long ago that I was a kid, Holly. It wasn't cavemen times. We had Lego. Action figures. Toy cars. Even computer games. Loads of things.'

'But none of it's here.'

'So we'll just have to improvise. How about I teach you a new card game?'

I shook my head.

'Or you could do some card tricks – you know, put on a magic show.'

'Here?'

'Why not?'

'Who'd be the audience? Oates? The woodland animals? The trees?'

'You could do a show for the best dad in the world.'

'When's he coming?'

'Ha. What about a show for Zeb and his dad? We could invite them over. They could bring nettle tea.'

I glared at him – just the thought of performing in front of Zeb and his dad was completely mortifying.

Then he smiled. 'Look – I was going to leave it till later in the week, but this might be a good time to get my I-pad out.'

I actually squealed with delight. But then he went to his rucksack, rummaged around, and pulled out a pad of A4 paper.

'Da-ad!'

'It's a pad,' he said. 'And it's mine. So – an "I-pad".'

I groaned.

'It's got plenty of apps,' he said. 'A paper-plane app. A drawing app. A writing app. Lots of games apps – hangman, boxes, noughts and crosses. We'll never be bored. And when we finish a page – we've got an instant fire-lighting app.'

Dad grinned. He thought he was hilarious. Lucky someone did.

7 The Stream

When I woke up the next morning, Dad was eating breakfast at the table, ripping off a hunk of crusty bread from a loaf and dipping it into a jar of honey. He'd put some bread on a plate for me, but after winding my pocket watch, I went straight for Wednesday's envelope, a light blue one, and tore it open.

Good morning, Holly!

Today's task: Pick a berry!

Make a boat!

Then float the berry across the stream!

Love, Mum.

P.S. Say hi to Dad and Oates from me. Hope they're not smelling too bad already!

'What's the task?' Dad asked, so I showed him the note. He smiled and said, 'The stream's a decent walk away – and, seeing how you got lost five minutes from here . . .'

I glared at him.

'. . . maybe I should come with you.'

'No, thanks,' I said. 'You get lost in supermarkets, remember?'

'It was a really big supermarket,' he said. 'There was an aisle just for cheese.'

'Still.'

'But you're not going alone,' he said. 'What about Zippy?'

'It's Zeb.'

'He might fancy an adventure, don't you think? With all that explorer-knowledge that he's got.'

'No, Dad.'

I'd be much too embarrassed to ask him, and besides, Mum's tasks were just for me.

But Dad said we should go over and say good morning to the neighbours anyway. 'It's only polite,' he insisted.

So after breakfast we all went over there – Dad and Oates enthusiastically. Me, not so much.

'Fancy tent,' whispered Dad, when we spotted it. It was red, green and silver, and had lots of zips. 'Not bad for cavemen.'

I gave him a look. A look that said, *Please don't embarrass me in front of these people again.*

'I'll behave,' he said. 'Scout's honour.' But then he shouted, 'Ahoy!' and Oates started barking his head off. I groaned.

Hearing the commotion, Hunter and Zeb popped up from behind the tent – where they'd been foraging, I guessed. Hunter looked a bit miffed to have his peace and quiet ruined, but Zeb seemed kind of pleased to see us.

'Did you sleep well?' Dad asked them.

'Yes, thanks,' said Hunter, 'but I've been up since five o'clock. Best part of the day.'

Dad had a fake-shocked expression. 'I didn't know there were two five o'clocks in the same day,' he said.

I looked at the ground. Did he have to make a joke about absolutely everything?

Then – just when I thought that he couldn't be any more embarrassing – he said, 'Holly and Oates are planning to go for a walk to the stream this morning – and I was wondering if Zeb would like to join them.'

My skin prickled. My face felt hot. How could he?

Zeb shrugged, nodded, and then he looked at his dad for permission.

'Well,' said Hunter, frowning, 'the whole idea of our break is actually to have a bit of man time, you see – away from the girls. No offence, young lady.'

I hated being called 'young lady' almost as much as I hated being called 'little girl'.

'But I wouldn't want you to get lost again, and Zeb kind of knows his way around – he's mostly capable outdoors, when he puts his brain in.' I glanced at Zeb, who rolled his eyes. 'So – sure,' Hunter said, like he was doing me a big favour.

Then he glanced at the sky, and we all looked up. There were only a few clouds.

'Feels like it might rain later,' he said.

'Really?' said Dad. 'Seems quite pleasant to me.'

Hunter wet a finger and held it up in the air. 'Something in the air pressure,' he announced. 'So don't be too long, guys.'

Zeb nodded, then he ducked inside the tent and came out wearing a fancy backpack and his red cap.

'Take a fishing rod and see if you can catch us some dinner,' Hunter said to him, but Zeb shook his head.

'I'm all right,' he said. 'Don't feel like fishing today.'

Hunter sighed deeply.

'See you kids later,' said Dad. 'Be good. Stay safe.'

I was tight-lipped and annoyed with both of the dads. It felt like neither of them trusted me to find the way on my own. So I started walking quickly in the direction of the stream, making sure that it was me who was leading the way.

When I looked back though, Zeb actually seemed really happy to be following, with Oates beside him.

Then, after a few minutes, Zeb called, 'Wait!' and I was sure that he was going to tell me we were going the wrong way. But when I spun around, he'd stopped and was pointing at the ground. At an animal dropping. Oates, of course, was sniffing it.

'If you're such an expert,' he said, smiling, 'what animal did that?' I walked over to it but I didn't have to get close to give him an answer. It ponged.

'A fox,' I said, and he chuckled. I was worried that he was making fun of me, but then he shook his head in amazement.

We stopped twice more – once so I could pick some dark red berries for the task and another time to use the compass on my pocket watch to check that we were going in the right direction.

I heard the trickle of the stream before I saw it. And when we got there, I felt super-proud.

The stream was wider than I'd imagined from the thin blue line on the map. It was as wide as a country road, but pretty shallow – only knee deep, even in the middle, and you could see the stones on the bottom. There was a gentle current and a soft burbling noise. It was incredibly peaceful.

Zeb stooped at the edge of the stream and sipped water from his cupped hands.

So I copied him. I was really thirsty from the walk and the water was deliciously cold – it chilled my hands and I could feel it sliding icily down my throat.

Oates lapped noisily at the water too, and Zeb pulled a large drink bottle from his backpack and filled it up from the stream. Then he sat down at the water's edge.

'So,' he said, 'why did you want to come here today?'

I was weighing up whether to tell him about the Mumbelievable Challenge. The cool thing to do was probably just shrug. The cool answer to everything was a shrug. Emily Fellows was a professional shrugger, pretty much. But now, instead of shrugging, I took Mum's note from my pocket and tentatively handed it to him. He unfolded the paper and read it.

'There's a task from Mum for every day of the holiday,' I explained, watching carefully for his reaction. I felt queasy, worried that he'd think the whole challenge was completely lame. But he smiled – just a little one, the tiniest upwards movement of his lips.

'Yesterday's task was to find five interesting things,' I said.

'The worm poo?'

I gave him an embarrassed grin and he smiled – a proper one this time.

'So let's try to make a boat,' he said.

'Um, no offence, but I should probably do it by myself. I mean, it might feel like cheating otherwise.'

He shrugged. I started gathering small sticks and plucking long blades of grass to tie them together. I'd been planning to make a tiny raft – the size of a hand – but it was incredibly fiddly and really frustrating.

Zeb, meanwhile, had collected some smooth flat pebbles and was now skimming them expertly down the stream. But when I launched my raft, with a berry balanced on top, he stopped and watched as I pushed it into the water.

It sank. Straight away. I sighed.

And so I went around collecting some more sticks – even lighter ones – for Raft Mark Two.

Zeb kept skimming pebbles until he ran out, and then he sat down and watched me trying to build the second raft.

'So, it's a family tradition?' I said. 'You and your dad camping – that's cool.'

He sighed and scratched at the dirt with a stick.

'The rest of the year I hardly see him. He and Mum split up when I was little. I go to boarding school, and my sisters and I mostly live with Mum in the holidays. We only stay with Dad every other weekend – if he's not busy with work, or off skiing with his girlfriend.

'He really spoils my sisters, but with me . . .' Zeb went quiet.

73

'What? Don't you get on?'

'He wants me to be a mini-version of him. He went to the same school. He was the captain of the rugby team – his name's on the honour board – and he tells me how he used to get *A*'s the whole time.'

I couldn't imagine Dad being like that with me. 'Do you *like* rugby?' I asked, because he didn't seem like the super-sporty type.

'No! And I'm not the smartest in the class, not even close. Plus –' he whispered the next bit – 'I don't really like camping either, to be honest. And I completely hate fishing.'

I couldn't help laughing, and this made him smile – a bit.

'But you know about explorers,' I said, confused.

'I like *reading* about them. I like reading about zombies too, but it doesn't mean that I want to *be* one. I've been completely dreading this trip,' he said. 'I'd rather be at home, with Mum and my sisters. They'll be shopping, or bowling, or going to the cinema – stuffing their faces with buckets of popcorn, eating ice cream. Meanwhile, I'm here eating berries and drinking nettle tea.'

74

'Does it sting – nettle tea?'

'No!' He smiled. 'It doesn't taste great though.'

'But your dad's actually pretty cool,' I pointed out. 'For a dad, I mean. He's like one of those survival guys off the telly. *My* dad's scared of everything. Snakes. Roller coasters. Clowns.'

'Clowns?'

'Really. Your dad seems completely fearless though.'

Zeb shook his head.

'He's terrified of Mum, for a start. And grizzly bears too, actually. Though he's never admitted the bear thing.'

'So how do you know?'

'Grandpa told me. They used to go camping when Dad was little, just the two of them, and one year they went hiking in this massive national park in the US and came face to face with a bear – and not a friendly one. They stood there, Grandpa and Dad, staring at the bear, and the bear stared back at them, until Grandpa – eventually – managed to scare it off.'

'Really? He frightened off a bear?'

'If you knew my grandpa,' Zeb explained, 'you wouldn't be surprised. But Dad just froze apparently –

he was scared stiff. Didn't speak for the rest of the day. Grandpa told me that, for years after, Dad had this complete bear-phobia. If there was a bear on TV, he'd have to leave the room. He even had nightmares about them.'

'Night-*bears*!' I said. 'Sorry. Dad joke.'

But Zeb smiled. 'Can I have a try?' he asked eventually. 'At making a boat?'

I nodded, because my second raft wasn't really happening, however hard I tried.

'Can you pass me the note?' he said.

I did, but instead of reading it, he started folding it – expertly, frowning in concentration, and in less than a minute he'd made a little origami boat.

'Wow,' I said, 'that's seriously good.'

He blushed. I took the boat from him, put the berry inside and carefully launched it.

It actually floated.

'Woo-hoo!'

But my joy was short-lived, because the paper boat wasn't floating *across* the stream, like the task had said. It was drifting *down*stream.

That's when Zeb did something kind of crazy. He pulled off his trainers and socks, frantically rolled up his jeans to above the knee, then waded into the stream and bent forward to try to blow the boat across. It worked – a bit. So I did the same – shoes and socks off, jeans rolled up – and splashed into the stream myself. The icy water on my legs! I gasped and then squealed! Luckily by now Zeb was squealing too. It was pretty funny. Together we chased the boat downstream and tried to blow it across – it was closer to the other bank now, but not quite there yet. And the stream was absolutely freezing.

That's when Oates decided to join in. He took a run-up and hurled himself into the water with a huge splash, soaking us.

'Oates!' I shrieked. 'Bad dog!'

But the wave that he'd created didn't only drench us – it had actually pushed the little paper boat to the other bank – it touched the side! We'd done it!

I whooped. So did Zeb, and he really didn't seem like a kid who'd had much whooping experience. We stomped out of the stream, dripping and shivering. Oates shook

himself dry, spraying us in the process, but we were already so wet we didn't care.

I'd wanted to do the task by myself, but I couldn't have done it without Zeb – and Oates! Plus, it was a lot more fun to be part of a team.

We laughed, and then tried to wring our clothes out without taking them off, which isn't easy, and we eventually gave up, put our socks and shoes back on, rolled down our wet jeans and started walking back. We hadn't even begun to dry out when the rain came.

8 Superman

The walk over to the stream had been pretty tiring, but the journey back was much slower. And squelchier.

It had been fun at first, with the thrum of the rain on leaves and all of us splashing in fresh puddles, but then it got cold and uncomfortable, and the rain was making it hard for us to figure out the way back.

I stopped a few times to check the compass – I'd thought that Zeb would have known the way for sure, but he seemed to be guessing too. And the longer we'd been going, with still no sign of the cabin, the surer I became that we were completely lost.

I was about to suggest that we should find a big tree to shelter under until the rain stopped, when Oates suddenly dashed off ahead of us. We tried to chase after him, weaving through trees, slipping in mud and blinking through the rain, when we saw – in front of us, at last – the cabin.

'Good boy, Oates!' I said, tingling with happiness and relief. 'Good dog!'

Then I noticed Dad.

He was standing outside the cabin. In the rain. And – except for his undies – he was completely naked.

His eyes were closed, and he was lathering shampoo into his hair and singing a song called 'Moon River'.

My dad was having a shower in the rain.

And, as if this wasn't bad enough, these were not just any undies that he was wearing – they were the Superman ones that Mum had bought him for Christmas. Zeb had stopped dead and was staring at Dad wide-eyed, like someone might stare at a yeti. I just wanted to disappear. Or for Dad to disappear – which would actually have been much better. But he didn't.

When Oates barked, Dad opened his eyes and saw us all gawping at him. A normal person might have looked embarrassed. But not Dad.

'I was beginning to worry about you two!'

'It really looks like it,' I said, shaking my head. 'Put some clothes on, will you?'

But he just grinned and carried on washing the bubbles out of his hair.

'You were the one who said I needed a shower, Lolly.'

I walked past him into the cabin, disgusted. Zeb followed, and then Oates too, who walked to the middle of the room and shook himself dry, spraying water on absolutely everything, including us. I sighed, picked up my towel and handed the other one – Dad's – to Zeb. We dried ourselves in front of the crackling fire.

'I'm really sorry about that,' I said, still blushing.

He shrugged and looked around.

'It's awesome in here,' he said. 'Wish we had a cabin like this.'

I smiled – a bit.

'Do you want a hot drink?' I asked him.

'As long as it's not made of nettles.'

'Hot chocolate?' I said, and a huge delighted look spread across Zeb's face, which made me smile too. But both of our smiles vanished when the door creaked open and the dads walked in.

Mine was still only wearing his pants, and was dripping wet, with a few shampoo bubbles still attached to his head. Zeb's was behind him, in blue waterproofs, and not looking at all pleased.

'I thought I warned you about the rain, Zeb,' he snapped.

Zeb looked like he was about to say something but then thought better of it.

'How about a nice hot drink while we all get dry?' Dad asked, but Hunter shook his head. He seemed incredibly disappointed with Zeb. Or maybe he was just finding it uncomfortable being in the same room as a man who was wearing a wet pair of Superman pants and absolutely nothing else. If he was, I knew exactly how he felt.

'Come on,' Hunter barked at Zeb. 'Let's go.'

Zeb handed me the towel, sighed and followed his dad out into the pouring rain.

9　Boothby Bennett

I changed out of my wet clothes into some fresh ones. Dad dried himself with the damp towel and put some actual clothes on. Then we both stood in front of the fire. The rain was still drumming loudly on the roof, so it was incredibly noisy, but in a way it was also dead quiet. Between us, I mean. Tense. Even Oates seemed to sense the atmosphere.

I didn't want to talk to Dad. I couldn't even look at him, couldn't trust myself not to explode.

'So, how was the task?' he asked eventually. 'Did you manage to do it before the rain came?'

I grunted.

'Is that a grunt for "yes" or a grunt for "no"?'

'*Yes.*'

He frowned.

'Have I done something wrong, Lolly?'

I stared at him, trying to work out if he was being serious.

He was being serious.

'You were outside,' I said, 'wearing pants – comedy pants – in front of a person I've just met. Do you understand just how embarrassing that is?'

He looked puzzled – he actually didn't get it.

'You also wrote a story for a national newspaper,' I added, 'about me running naked around a hotel.'

Dad sighed. 'Look, Lolly – I'm really sorry about that. But you were just a cute little kid back then. It was supposed to embarrass *me*, not you – it was meant to be, you know, light-hearted, funny.'

I bit my lip to stop myself crying.

'You think that it was funny for me at school? "Holly's a nudie." "Holly's a streaker." "Aren't you a bit hot, Holly, with all those clothes on?"'

Dad winced and took a deep breath – he seemed to understand, at last.

'I'm sorry, Lol—'

'It's Holly,' I snapped. 'I'm not a little kid any more! And I just want to go home!'

Oates yapped nervously. He did this whenever there was an argument – to try to stop it – but he always ended up making things worse.

And I wasn't ready to finish yet.

'And you're always away! You missed my birthday *and* the talent show! It's like your writing's more important than your family!'

'Oh, that's just not true, Holly.'

Dad made a move to give me a hug, but I shook my head and glared fiercely at him to back off. Then I went over to the bottom bunk and curled up under the blanket.

Not long after, Oates padded over, sniffed me and then breathed on me with his doggy breath. He was only trying to be helpful, but it really wasn't.

A few minutes later, Dad came over with a steaming mug of hot chocolate and, when I didn't move, he left it on the floor beside the bed. I wanted to ignore it, but it just smelled too delicious.

So I wriggled out from under the blanket, sat up in bed and leaned forward to pick up the mug. There was a coaster underneath – a folded-up piece of paper with 'Open Me' written on it. Reluctantly, I unfolded it.

In the evening, the atmosphere inside the cabin was stuffy and I was still pretty grumpy. Oates was keeping out of the way. I read my book. Dad did some writing, kept the fire going and cooked dinner, which was two-minute noodles. (Dad always joked that he was such a good cook he could make two-minute noodles in one minute, forty-five seconds.)

After dinner Dad suggested a game of cards, but I really wasn't in the mood. The rain had stopped by now, so I went outside to get some fresh air. Oates followed me, glad of the break. It was still cloudy and the light was fading, the ground damp, everything soggy.

I looked in the direction of Zeb's tent and wondered what he would be doing right now. I felt sorry for him, stuck in a little tent with his dad. Maybe Zeb felt sorry for me too, stuck in a cabin with mine.

I watched Oates run around for a while. He was bounding with excitement and chasing after insects as if he'd just invented a brilliant new game. He sniffed each new tree like he was the first dog to discover it. Maybe he was.

I wished that I could be more like Oates – not the

whole sniffing-bottoms thing, or the random barking either, or the licking. And definitely not all the weeing. But, you know, his *enthusiasm*. 'Living in the moment,' Mum called it. Oates wasn't the cleverest dog, but he was a complete expert at that, so maybe he was smart after all.

I wished that I could shake off a bad mood like Oates shook off water. But I just couldn't. Not recently, anyway.

Even my book couldn't cheer me up, and I was in bed before eight o'clock. Oates was exhausted too, resting by the fire. Dad sat at the table for a bit, writing in the flickering candlelight, as if he was Shakespeare or something, but soon he scraped back his chair, sighed and clambered up to the top bunk. Noisily. Dad never did anything quietly. When he ate noodles, it sounded like bathwater gurgling down a plughole.

'Are you awake, Holly?' he asked in a loud whisper – he even *whispered* loudly. I grunted – because if I hadn't been awake before, I certainly would have been now. 'Wanna hear a story?' he said.

I grunted again.

'That's a "yes" grunt, right?'

I sighed.

'It's not going to be a scary one, is it?' I muttered.

'Oh, no. No, no, no, no. Yes. A bit. Maybe.'

'*Dad.*'

He cleared his throat – noisily.

'I did an internet search about this cabin,' he said. 'Before we left. It's got an interesting history all right. It was actually built by a girl and her dad, many years ago – a highly adventurous ten-year-old girl, and her very handsome, super-nice, super-hilarious dad. Oh, and a dog with only very basic personal hygiene.'

I groaned and, with perfect timing, Oates farted in

his sleep. Dad hooted with laughter. Even I had to smile.

'They built this place with their own hands,' Dad continued, 'using trees from the forest, and they lived here very happily – although the dad could, on occasion, be incredibly embarrassing. And the girl, also very occasionally, could be just a tiny bit moody.'

I groaned again.

'Yes,' he said, 'exactly like that. Now one day – one very wet day, much like today – a man came into the woods. A strange man with wild hair, a straggly beard and mean little eyes. That man's name was – Boothby Bennett.'

I snorted. I couldn't help myself. It was a completely ridiculous name to choose, even by Dad's standards.

'You're not, I hope, laughing at Boothby Bennett's name,' said Dad, in his pretend-serious voice, 'because no one can be blamed for their name. Not even Boothby Bennett. Like many things in life, you can only blame the parents.

'Now, you might be wondering why Boothby Bennett was out alone in these woods, at night, so very far away from everything.'

'No, I wasn't wondering at all,' I said, because I didn't want to make it easy for Dad. I didn't want to let him think that he could just make me laugh with a silly cartoon and a daft bedtime story and that everything would suddenly be okay.

'Take a wild guess,' said Dad, 'why a man – why Boothby Bennett – might be walking in these woods all by himself.'

'He liked nature?' I guessed unenthusiastically.

'Not one bit,' said Dad. 'He absolutely hated nature. Hated most things in fact. Hated people. Plants. Puppies. He even hated mint-choc-chip ice cream, and you should never trust someone who hates mint-choc-chip ice cream. No, the truth was, Boothby Bennett was on the run. From the police. He was a fugitive.'

Dad left a really long silence, and I just couldn't help myself from asking the obvious question.

'What had he done?'

'What *hadn't* he done?' said Dad. 'He'd committed every crime in the book, and plenty that weren't in the book. Theft. Burglary. Littering. Kidnapping. Dadnapping, which is like kidnapping but with a—'

'*Dad.*'

'Exactly. And he'd also committed the very worst crime of all. He . . . didn't brush his teeth.'

'*Dad!*'

'I'm serious, Holly. Not once. Not even that thing that you do sometimes, where you pretend to brush your teeth but you're really just smearing a bit of toothpaste around so that you've got minty-fresh breath. He'd *never* brushed his teeth. His breath smelled worse than Oates's. Worse, indeed, than Ernest's nappies. Worse even – than Mum's lentil lasagne.'

'I'm telling Mum . . .'

'Now, on the night in question, a night very much like tonight, Boothby Bennett was tired and cold and lost, when he spotted this very cabin here. There was a wisp of smoke coming from the chimney and a faint flickering light through the curtains. The girl and her dad were lying in their bunk beds. And then . . .'

Knock, knock!

I screamed!

Oates scrambled to his feet, yapping.

But Dad was giggling.

'Sorry,' he said. 'It was just me.'

I grunted, furious. My heart was still doing a drum roll. I was out of breath.

'You said it wasn't going to be a scary one.'

Then –

Knock-knock! Knock-knock! Louder this time.

'Was that you?' Dad asked.

'No,' I snapped. 'It was you again. You must think I'm . . .'

KNOCK-KNOCK. Even louder – and it definitely wasn't Dad. It was coming from the door.

I screamed again.

And this time, so did Dad.

10 Missing

As Dad leapt down from the top bunk, I sprang up from mine, and we only just avoided crashing into each other. I held my breath and grabbed Dad's arm.

'Who's there?' said Dad, panting heavily.

'Zeb,' came the muffled voice from outside.

I sighed with relief. Oates barked.

When Dad unlocked the door and opened it, we had to shield our eyes from the dazzling light – Zeb had a little torch strapped onto his head, the kind of light that miners wear on their helmets. He must have seen us squinting, because he clicked it off and apologised.

'You scared the absolute pants off us,' Dad said, as if anyone needed reminding about Dad's pants.

'It's my dad,' said Zeb, shaking his head. 'He went out hours ago and hasn't come back.'

'Come on in,' said Dad.

Zeb stepped inside and Dad closed the door behind him. The candle was still flickering on the table, and the fire was still going, just, so there was enough light to see that Zeb was really upset.

'He went to get some food for dinner – catch a fish from the stream, he said. But that was hours ago –' Zeb glanced at his digital watch – 'four hours and twenty minutes. He said that he'd be back in two.'

'Maybe he was finding it hard to catch something,' Dad suggested, 'and didn't want to come back empty-handed. Maybe he just lost track of time.'

Zeb shook his head.

'Not Dad. Not ever. Everything's always to schedule. He's never late. If I'm five minutes late for something, he gets really mad. No – something must have happened to him.'

'We don't know that,' said Dad gently. 'And your dad looks like he can take care of himself out there.'

'That's exactly what I'm saying,' said Zeb, getting frustrated now. 'For him not to come back, something really bad must have happened.' He pulled another torch from his pocket, the same kind that he was wearing, the kind that you strap around your head. 'He didn't take this with him, or either of the spare torches. So he must have planned on being back at the tent before sunset. He'd never make that kind of mistake.'

'What if he comes back to the tent right now?' Dad asked.

'I left him a note to say that I'd be here – and a spare torch so that he can read the note.'

Dad looked like he was thinking really hard. And then he nodded. He'd made a decision.

'Zeb, you stay here with Holly and Oates. I bet you're starving, aren't you?'

Zeb nodded.

'Holly will take care of the fire and get you something to eat and drink. Can I borrow your dad's torch?'

Zeb passed it to him.

'So, he went to the stream?' Dad asked. 'You're sure about that?'

Zeb nodded. 'He took his fishing stuff.'

'Right,' said Dad. 'I'll go and find him then.'

Dad's voice was unusually manly, like he was a hero from a movie and not a man who had once got lost in a supermarket.

'Can I leave you in charge, Holly?'

I nodded.

He kissed me on top of my head, and this time I actually didn't mind.

Then he ruffled Oates's fur, said goodbye to Zeb and

stepped outside, closing the door firmly behind him.

Zeb and I stood there in awkward silence for a few moments. Then I handed him a muesli bar, which he tore open and ate hungrily. So I gave him another one, and a handful of dried apricots too.

Then I put more wood on the fire, filled the pot with water and hung it up to boil.

I was feeling a bit weird: it was like I was happy and sad at the same time. Of course, I wasn't happy that Zeb's dad was missing – not at all – or that Zeb was upset, or that Dad was outside in the dark. But I was feeling proud to have been put in charge. It felt like Dad was trusting me to be grown up. And here in the cabin, just me and Zeb, it felt nice too, like a sleepover.

I sat at the table, and Zeb sat down and stared blankly into the fire.

'Dad says that a real fire's better than TV,' he mumbled.

'My dad says that too. There must be a dads' club, where they learn lame jokes and a whole load of annoying things to say.' Zeb smiled – a bit. 'It's not though, is it?' I said. 'Not better than the telly.'

'Not even close,' he said. Then he sighed.

'What's up?' I asked him.

'Dad was in a real mood with me when he left, because I'd got caught in the rain, even though he'd warned me, and because I hadn't wanted to catch a fish. I can't seem to get anything right.' He sighed deeply again, then said, 'Your parents are great.'

I frowned – he'd never met my mum, and he *had* met my dad.

'I don't know about that,' I said.

'Your mum gives you fun tasks to do while you're on holiday . . .'

'. . . and my dad has showers in the rain wearing Superman pants,' I added, blushing.

'He's funny,' said Zeb, with a shrug.

'Funny peculiar,' I said.

'Nope – funny *funny*.'

'Here's the thing about having a funny dad,' I said, and then I told him about the newspaper story of my hotel nudie-run. It was probably the single most embarrassing thing that I could have said, and I found myself blushing the whole way through it, but he was actually grinning,

so I was happy that I'd said it – it seemed to take his mind off his worries for a moment at least.

The water had boiled by now and I ladled it out into the mugs, then mixed in the chocolate powder with a spoon. We sat silently for a while, blowing on our drinks, savouring the chocolatey smell and letting the steam warm our faces.

Then Zeb was starting to look anxious again, and I bombarded him with questions so that he could think about something other than his missing dad. I asked him about his house (his mum's was big, with a huge garden, and his dad's was a small apartment with all the latest gadgets and a huge telly). I asked if he had any pets (his mum had a labradoodle called Arthur and his sisters had two guinea pigs called Bubble and Squeak). His sisters were fifteen and fourteen, and their hobbies were shopping, whispering, arguing and karate. I asked him about his school, and he told me the name: St Swithin's Boys' Academy.

'Sounds a bit posh,' I said. He shrugged. 'Only boys? That's a complete nightmare. I bet there's a lot of farting.'

'There is,' he admitted.

'I bet you have a posh uniform too,' I said, and he blushed. 'What?'

'You'll laugh,' he said.

'I won't.'

'We wear boater hats and stripy blazers.'

He was right – I burst out laughing. I actually snorted. I just couldn't help it.

'What colour are the stripes?'

'Blue, green, orange.'

I laughed again. So did he this time.

'That's completely mental,' I said. 'How can you even concentrate on the lessons, with all those colours clashing?'

'What's *your* school like?' he said, to change the subject.

I told him about the nice things (Ms Devenport, Asha, geography lessons) and the not-so-nice things (Emily Fellows and her gang, all the teasing, Mr Fisher's coffee breath). Then Zeb told me about a boy at his school called Robin Collins-Roberts, whose name was a real tongue-twister and who seemed like a male version of Emily Fellows, except that he was posher and was a world-class giver of wedgies.

We both went quiet for a bit, trying to listen out for our dads – and then we stood up, opened the door and stepped outside – partly to look out for them, and partly for the cool breeze. Oates went for a wee, just for something to do.

We stood outside in the darkness for a minute or two and, hearing nothing but insects and Oates and the occasional hoot of an owl, we went back inside and sat down again. I was really tired by now – my head kept lolling forward, but I was much too jittery to sleep.

I looked at my pocket watch. Dad had been out there for an hour and thirty-two minutes.

One hour and three-quarters.

Two hours.

Zeb scraped the chair back, stood up and said, 'I've got to go and look for him myself.'

I knew that I should have tried to talk him out of it. Or at least said that I would stay here, in case the dads came back.

But I didn't, because I knew how he felt. My dad had been gone for two hours, which felt like long enough, but Zeb's dad had been missing for more than six hours now – in the dark, without a torch.

So I stood up too. I couldn't let him go out there alone, and we couldn't just wait here any more, not while our dads might be in danger.

I scribbled a quick note on Dad's 'I-pad' and left it on the table:

We've gone looking for you and Hunter.
Back soon.
Holly x

'Oates!' I said. 'Come on, boy!'

He'd been dozing, but now he sprang into action.

Zeb took a small torch from his pocket, passed it to me and fixed his own torch to his head. Then we stepped out into the darkness.

'For cavemen,' I said, 'you really do have a lot of torches.'

Zeb rolled his eyes.

Perhaps I was more like my dad than I'd realised.

11   Into the Woods

We stumbled over to Zeb's tent in the weak light of our torches, to make sure that his dad hadn't come back. He hadn't.

Zeb scribbled on the note he'd written to his dad, to say that we'd gone out looking for him but that we'd be back soon. Then, outside the tent, Zeb crouched and studied the ground and eventually made out a faint trail of his dad's muddy footprints. We followed them for a few minutes, step by careful step, until we  completely lost the trail over rocky ground, but we kept on going in what we guessed was the right direction – to the stream.

It had been hard enough to find our way through the woods in the daytime. In the dark, it was almost impossible.

It was noisier at night too. In the day there was birdsong, but at night there was the buzzing and clicking of thousands of insects, the sad hoots of owls and the strange croaking and burping of frogs.

Oates barked every time he heard the rustling of an animal, which was quite a lot. I was pretty jumpy too; not

knowing what each creature might be, or where it was –
it was incredibly creepy. You couldn't tell what might be
lurking nearby.

Every minute or so, one of us would yell 'Dad!', but
there was no answer. Not even an echo.

When Zeb stopped suddenly and let out a groan,
I thought he must have hurt himself: twisted an ankle,
scraped his leg on something or walked into a tree. But it
turned out that he'd just had enough.

'We're completely lost,' he muttered. 'This was a
stupid idea. Stupid, stupid, stupid.'

I shone the torch at my pocket watch. We'd only been
going for twenty-five minutes, though it did feel like much
longer.

'They're out here somewhere,' I said.

'Where though?'

I couldn't answer that, of course. My first thought
had been that Zeb's dad had got injured – a broken leg
or something like that, and my Dad was struggling to
bring him back to our cabin. My other thoughts were that
Hunter had slipped over and hit his head, or that he'd
fallen into some kind of hole.

But the more I thought about it, the more all of these things seemed pretty unlikely. Hunter was a survival expert after all. *My* dad was the type of person who might trip over, be knocked unconscious or plummet into a hole. Not Zeb's dad.

Zeb was looking scared and upset, and I was feeling the same way. But we had to keep going.

I shone the torch at the compass part of my pocket watch and, when I was pretty sure I had the right direction, I turned to Zeb and said, 'Follow me.'

I sounded a lot more confident than I felt, and I had no idea what I would do if he didn't follow me. Oates came straight away, but Zeb was hesitating, then he grunted, and finally he came after us.

A long time later there was still no sign of either dad, and no sign of the stream that we were heading for either. I was completely exhausted. Even Oates seemed out of breath. Zeb was wheezing too, and hadn't spoken for ages – until he shouted, 'Stop!'

When I spun around and pointed the torch at him, he was crouching and staring at a large footprint.

'It's my dad's!' he said. Then he sprang up and yelled, 'Dad!'

We held our breath.

Still no answer.

But it felt as if we were on the right track at least. Zeb took the lead again – the footprint had given him a new burst of energy. I hurried after him. Oates too.

'Dad!' shouted Zeb.

This time a faint sound came back.

'Zeb?!'

It was Hunter's voice, coming from a long way off, and he was shouting something else too, something that neither of us could make out. Zeb rushed towards the sound of his voice, stumbling and scraping branches, and I tried to keep up.

'Dad!' Zeb shouted.

'Over here!' yelled Hunter. We could hear him clearly now. 'Climb a tree, son! Climb a tree!'

'What?'

'Climb the nearest tree!' There was real fear in his voice. 'There's a bear!' he yelled.

Zeb stopped dead. I did too – right behind him.

'A what?' yelled Zeb.

'A bear!' Hunter repeated, in a panicky voice.

Zeb looked around, and I spun around with my torch too. Nothing. No sign of any animals, let alone a bear.

'A bear?' Zeb shouted. 'Are you sure?'

'I swear!' Hunter yelled back.

'Where?'

'Out there!'

'Where, out there?'

'Somewhere!'

They were starting to sound like a book by Dr Seuss, so I tugged Zeb's sleeve.

'But there aren't any, are there?' I said. 'Not in the entire country!'

'Where is it, Dad?' Zeb shouted. 'This bear.'

'I don't know! It's dark!'

'So how did you see it then?'

'It was light back then!' Hunter snapped. 'Climb a tree, Zeb! Now! Save yourself! It's not safe down there!'

'Where *are* you?'

'Up a tree! Over here!'

When we reached Hunter's tree, we looked up into

the branches. Hunter was halfway up, sitting on a thick branch and gripping the trunk like a wrestling hold.

I recognised the look on his face – it was like he wanted to move but his body just wouldn't. His eyes were wild with fear. I'd felt exactly the same when I'd climbed the tree in our garden for the Dadventure – I'd been so completely terrified of heights then.

'Something might have snapped in his mind,' Zeb muttered. 'Grandpa said that Dad freaked out in a toyshop once, when he was a kid. All those teddies reminded him of that bear. I think it's happening again.'

'But what made him snap?' I asked. 'What did he see that he thought was a bear?'

'Your dad?' suggested Zeb.

I shook my head. Dad was slightly hairy, but not particularly bear-like, except when he was eating. And besides, Hunter said he'd seen the bear when it was still light, and he'd been missing since long before Dad went looking for him. So what could he have seen that terrified him so much that he'd bolted up a tree and stayed there? It just didn't make any sense. Unless . . .

I pointed my torch at the ground and looked around,

like a detective searching for clues.

That's when I saw it – not far from the tree. Something on the ground. An animal dropping, but no ordinary one. This was a huge mound. Fresh too. I knew Oates's poos well – much too well, in fact. But this was much too big to have been him.

I crouched and looked closer.

'Zeb, come here!' I whispered. 'I think –' I could hardly believe what I was about to say – 'I think this might actually be from a bear.'

Zeb gasped and immediately started looking for tracks. He soon found some.

'Bear?' I said.

'Hard to say – but they're big enough, and I don't recognise them. So ...'

My first reaction – strangely – was relief: that Zeb's dad hadn't been imagining things. But then, a moment later, my entire body tensed up. If there was an actual bear in the woods, where was he right now? And where was Dad? My chest tightened, and I could hardly breathe.

'Dad!' I shrieked. 'Dad!'

Then, just when I thought things couldn't possibly get any worse, Oates bolted off, barking.

'Oates!' I yelled. 'Come back!'

But there was a rustle of long grass, and Oates was gone.

12 Un-bear-lievable

I'd wanted a real adventure for as long as I could remember. But this was too real. There was a bear in the woods. Possibly. Probably. And my dad was missing. Oates had abandoned me, Zeb was trembling and his dad was up a tree.

I gripped my torch and tried to stay calm. I couldn't think. Could hardly breathe.

Then – a distant bark. Was that . . . Oates? I listened carefully. Another bark, and then a shout, very faint but completely unmistakable!

'Holly?!'

'Dad?!' I yelled.

'I'm coming, Holly!'

I moaned with relief and then waved my torch around excitedly, yelling, 'Over here! Dad – there's a bear!'

Oates bounded over and almost knocked me down. It was another minute before Dad reached us and, when he did, his hug was a real bone-cruncher, as if he hadn't seen me for weeks, so I could hardly get my words out. 'There's a bear, Dad!'

He let go and frowned at me.

'Don't be silly. And didn't I tell you to wait in the cabin?'

He didn't seem angry though – just confused.

My words tumbled out. 'We did wait, for ages – then we couldn't wait any more. We thought you must be lost...'

'I was – a bit,' he said, looking sheepish.

I pointed the torch up at the tree.

'We found Zeb's dad ...'

'What are you doing up there?' Dad shouted up.

'Bear!' yelled Hunter. 'Have you all completely lost your minds?! There's a bear out there!'

'But there aren't any bears here,' Dad pointed out, as if *we'd* all lost our minds.

'That's what *we* said,' I explained breathlessly, 'but there's a huge poo over there, which could be a bear's, and big tracks, too big for a dog or anything like that.'

I shone the torch at the ground to show him.

Dad crouched, then looked at me wide-eyed and took a deep breath.

'You might actually be right,' he said.

'They *are* right!' yelled Hunter, more desperately than ever. 'Save yourselves – climb a tree!'

'Can't bears climb trees though?' asked Dad. 'Koala bears can definitely climb – that's for sure.'

'A koala's not a bear, Dad.'

'Winnie the Pooh can climb,' he said. 'To get honey. What type of bear is *he*?'

'A made-up one?'

I sighed. Dad really wasn't helping. But then he actually did – help, I mean.

He asked me and Zeb to shine our torches at the base of the tree, and then – very awkwardly – he started climbing. When he reached Hunter, I couldn't hear what they were saying, but Dad was obviously trying to talk him down. At first Hunter was shaking his head a lot, but my dad was really persistent, as usual, and Hunter eventually gave up – he nodded, loosened his grip on the tree and followed Dad as he edged down the trunk.

Now that he was back on the ground, Hunter looked terrified and kept glancing nervously around.

Dad put his hand on Hunter's shoulder. 'We really need your help here, mate,' he said. 'To get us back to the log cabin, and safety.'

Dad took off his head-torch and passed it to Hunter, who put it on, took a deep breath and led the way – snaking through the trees towards the cabin. We all

124

followed. My whole body was aching, but I'd never been more alert, never more on edge. No matter how tired you are, the thought of a bear stalking you will wake you up pretty quickly.

With Hunter leading the way, Dad at the back and Oates getting in everyone's way, we weaved around trees and over rocks, stumbling, groaning, panting. Every rustle of grass and every snap of a twig was terrifying: every noise might be a bear!

When we finally saw the cabin in front of us – a joyous sight! – we all hurtled towards it. Hunter was first – he flung the door open and checked inside. No bears. So we piled in, and Dad – the last one in – locked the door behind us. We all looked at each other, completely out of breath.

I'm not sure who it was that started laughing first. It might even have been me. But we were so incredibly relieved that soon we were all in hysterics, doubled over. Oates was barking. He probably had no idea what was going on. Or maybe he just wanted to join in.

When the laughter died out, Zeb said, 'Now what? We're trapped in a cabin, with a bear out there, and with no way of getting help.'

He was right.

'We just sit tight, I guess,' said Dad.

'Until?' I asked.

Dad shrugged.

'Until the bear goes, I suppose.'

'Or until we run out of food,' I said, 'and we have to start eating each other.'

'And, anyway,' said Zeb, 'how will we know when the bear has gone?'

There was an awkward silence.

'That's a good point,' Dad said. 'If only we had a phone. To call for help.'

Hunter suddenly looked incredibly sheepish. 'I've got one,' he said. 'It's in my bag, in the tent.'

Zeb was shaking his head in disbelief. '"Survive like cavemen," you said. You made me drink nettle tea! And you had a phone all along?'

'I needed to send some texts to my work, Zeb – I only ever used it first thing in the morning, before you woke up. Then I switched it off.' And then, as if he'd decided to confess everything, he added, 'The phone is how I knew it would rain today – I checked the weather app.' He looked really uncomfortable – super-embarrassed. Then he said, 'I'll go and get it now.'

'No,' said Dad. 'Way too dangerous.'

Hunter shook his head. 'It's like you said up the tree – I've got to face my fears.'

'Facing your fears is a good thing, it's true,' said Dad, 'but leaving the safety of the cabin to go out and face *bears* – that's a really dumb idea.'

But Hunter stepped past Dad, unlocked the door and

dashed outside. 'Don't go, Dad!' yelped Zeb, but it was too late.

We all stood in silence at the open door. Zeb and I were shining our torches and listening for the bear. We could hardly breathe.

13 Emergency

My ears had never been more sensitive – not even those times in class when Emily Fellows was whispering about me.

As we stood on the front step of the cabin, there was just the clicking of insects, the rustle of the wind in the leaves and the sound of our breathing. When I heard fast footsteps coming our way, I froze, not knowing if it was Hunter or the bear.

It was Hunter, sprinting back, clutching the phone, like a relay runner with a baton. We all sighed with relief.

When he reached us, we bolted back inside and Dad locked the door.

'Let's make extra-sure it can't get in,' he said. 'Bears

have a very powerful sense of smell. He might be able to sniff us out. Or sniff out our food.'

I wasn't sure how accurate this information was – Dad had thought that a koala was a bear after all – but it really wasn't worth taking any chances. So we all got to work, dragging the bunk beds over to the door, and then the table and chairs to prop up against the bunk beds. Finally, with Hunter still out of breath from his dash to the tent, Dad took the mobile from him, dialled and put it on speakerphone. There was a woman's voice.

'Which emergency service do you require?'

'Well, I'm not really sure,' said Dad. 'I want to report a bear, please.'

'A bear?'

'Yep.'

The woman hesitated.

'And you're reporting the bear for doing what, exactly, sir?'

'For being in the woods,' Dad said. The woman groaned, as if she was used to getting prank calls, so Dad added, 'Really – there's a bear on the loose, in Fir Forest.'

'You do realise, sir, that it's a serious offence to make false reports.'

'Yes,' said Dad, 'but—'

'And is it only the one bear, sir, or are there three of them – a mummy, a daddy and a baby, with bowls of porridge at a range of temperatures?'

'I'm completely serious,' said Dad. 'There's an actual bear. On the loose.'

'You saw this bear with your own eyes, sir?'

'Yes. Well, no,' he admitted, '*I* didn't, but someone did – he's here with me – and my daughter identified the – um – the *dropping*.'

'The dropping?'

'The poo,' said Dad. 'The bear poo.'

There was another very awkward silence.

'Your daughter is able to identify animal droppings?' she asked.

'She actually is,' said Dad proudly. 'She's a real expert.'

But the woman still wasn't convinced.

'What kind of bear was it? Grizzly? Polar? Teddy?'

'Grizzly,' said Hunter firmly.

'It's dark outside,' said the woman. 'Do you think you might have mistaken another animal for a bear? A large rabbit, say?'

'A three-metre high rabbit with huge paws?' snapped Hunter. 'I don't think so, madam. Look – I've got plenty of survival experience, and I know what I saw. The tracks too. Unmistakable.'

'To recap,' said the woman, 'you're reporting a three-metre high grizzly bear, in Fir Forest.'

'That's right,' said Dad impatiently.

The woman sighed. 'Can I have your details then, sir?'

Dad gave her his name and then both addresses – our home one, and our address right here, which was 'The Cabin in the Woods, Fir Forest'.

When the call ended, we all just stood there, not sure what to do now. Because if nobody believed us, we were stuck here. Completely stuck.

'Maybe it wasn't a bear,' said Dad eventually, like he was trying to convince himself. 'Maybe it was just another big animal. A harmless one. Or a man in a bear costume.'

Hunter shook his head. 'I know what I saw.'

Seconds later we all jolted as the phone rang.

'Hello?' said Dad breathlessly.

It was the same woman, but she wasn't being sarcastic any more.

'Whatever you do, don't leave the cabin! A bear has just been reported missing from the safari park. Are you safe where you are?'

'Yes,' said Dad. 'I think so.'

'The cabin is secure?'

'I guess. It's made of wood, which isn't as safe as bricks obviously, but it's much better than straw –

at least, according to the three little pigs.'

I shook my head in disbelief – there really was no situation where Dad wouldn't try to make a completely stupid joke.

'Can you give us any more details, sir? About your position, and about where the bear was sighted, and when. We're despatching a helicopter right now.'

Dad told her everything that he knew, which wasn't much, and Hunter chipped in with more details.

'Stay inside,' the woman said. 'The missing bear is called Barney, but don't be fooled by the friendly name. According to the safari-park manager, he's got a real temper. They don't even let him mix with the other bears. On no account should he be approached.'

'We weren't planning on it,' said Dad.

When the phone call ended, there was another silence, until Zeb said, 'I'm sorry, Dad. Sorry that I didn't believe you.'

Dad and I apologised too.

'No – *I'm* the one who should be saying sorry,' said Hunter. 'For hiding up a tree like a complete coward, when I should have been making sure that you were all safe.'

Dad shook his head.

'Fear makes us do strange things,' he said. 'No one knows what they would do if they were face to face with a clown, until it happens.'

We all looked at Dad.

'Did I say "clown"? I meant "bear" of course.'

This gave me an idea. Dad was right – about bears, I mean. None of us really knew what to do if it came looking for us, but we did have a book that might help. I picked up Dad's pocket survival guide.

SURVIVAL: IN EVENT OF BEAR ATTACK

1 PLAY DEAD

ROAR!! 2 MAKE NOISE

53

'Well, playing dead is definitely the easiest option,' said Zeb.

'Not for Oates it isn't,' I pointed out.

'Isn't playing dead one of those things that most dogs are good at, like sitting and fetching?'

'Oates isn't most dogs. He's either asleep, or running around, or weeing. He doesn't do acting.'

'So option two it is then,' said Dad calmly, like he was choosing an item from a menu. 'Who's up for a mug of hot chocolate?'

We all were.

Luckily we had plenty of wood. Dad and Hunter built up the fire, and then we all sat on the floor in front of it, eating the last of the dried apricots and trying not to think about the bear.

While we were waiting for the water to boil, I carefully tore out some sheets from Dad's 'I-pad' and asked Zeb to teach me how to make a boat. It wasn't as easy as he'd made it look, but by the second go I'd kind of got the hang of it. Then he showed me how to make a small box and, finally, a frog, though the frog was really tricky and mine ended up looking more like a toad that had been squished by a truck.

Hunter had been watching Zeb teach me origami.

'Wow. Where did you learn to do *that*, son? At school?'

'From the internet,' Zeb said.

'That's brilliant,' Hunter said, and Zeb frowned, and then smiled, as if it had been a really long time since he'd received a compliment from his dad.

'Speaking of brilliant,' my dad said, 'you really should see some of Holly's magic.'

I gave him a look – this was the same Dad, remember, who only hours earlier had promised me that he'd try to be less embarrassing.

'Go on, Holly,' he said. 'Show us a trick.'

'Come on,' said Zeb. 'I love magic.'

Even Hunter joined in, chanting my name and stomping his feet.

So I did a card trick, and it went well – they all clapped, anyway.

'How did you do that?' said Zeb, shaking his head in wonder.

'I could tell you,' I said, 'but then I'd have to kill you.'

Dad thought that this was hilarious.

The water was bubbling away in the pot by now, and Dad made the hot chocolate. There were only two mugs, so Dad and I had to share one, and Zeb and Hunter shared the other.

The helicopter arrived – I could hear it coming from way off, above the crackle of the fire, and the noise got louder and louder until it passed right overhead and was completely deafening, louder than anything I'd heard in my life. Louder than Ernest wailing. Louder even than Harrison Duffy's farts.

The helicopter rattled the entire cabin and everything inside. We all covered our ears. I could see that Oates was barking his head off, but I couldn't hear him at all over the ear-splitting *wokka-wokka-wokka* of the blades. The helicopter's searchlight, when it passed over the cabin, lit up the whole place, and then it zoomed off to look for the bear.

When it was far enough away that we could hear each other again, I said, 'What will they do when they find it? Kill it?'

I really, really hoped not, no matter how bad-tempered Barney was.

'Tranquilliser gun,' said Hunter. 'They'll fire a dart at him, if they can, and put him to sleep. And then they'll bundle him up in a net and take him back home. But first, of course, they'll have to find him. And bears would be absolute experts at hiding in woods.'

'Meanwhile,' Dad said, to change the subject again, 'our talent show continues.' He frowned mischievously at Hunter. 'Your son's a genius at origami. Holly's fantastic at magic. So, what's your special talent, I wonder?'

Hunter seemed to give this a lot of thought, and then – while we were all staring at him in anticipation – he wiggled his ears. It was hilarious. Then he crossed his eyes. More laughter, most of it from me: other people's dads are nearly always less embarrassing than your own.

Zeb was shaking his head though, and going a bit red.

'Don't do the pec thing, Dad,' he said, but this was obviously the wrong thing to say, because Hunter grinned, took off his top and started flexing his chest muscles – in time to a song that he was whistling. It was super-hilarious – Dad and I were hooting with laughter. I gave Zeb a raised-eyebrow look and a smile – to mean,

Maybe you do *have a cool dad after all.*

Zeb, however, had turned a very deep shade of red by now. Hunter, much to Zeb's relief, put his top back on and smiled at Dad.

'Your turn, buddy. What's your talent?'

'Well,' said Dad, 'I was planning to do exactly what you just did –' we all laughed – 'but now I suppose I'll have to think of something else. Hmm. Well, I could always do a song, I suppose.'

And I was thinking, *Please, not the sausage song. Anything but the sausage song.*

'It's called the sausage song,' Dad said. I groaned. Zeb giggled. And Dad started singing, in a deep voice, like an opera singer.

'I had a sausage
A lovely little sausage
And I put it in the oven for my tea.
I went down to the cellar
To fetch my um-ber-ella
And the sausage came after me.'

Zeb seemed to find it all hilarious, and Hunter was grinning too. But I was blushing and wanting it all to end. Immediately. At least before the second verse.

But you should always be careful what you wish for. Dad did stop singing straight away – because there was a massive thud. Something hitting the wall.

The cabin shook, but this time it wasn't because of the helicopter. We all spun around, towards the noise, holding our breath. No one dared say a word.

Then, from outside – a heart-stopping roar.

14 Pursued by a Bear

Dad snatched up the phone from the floor and scrambled to his feet – we all did – and called the emergency services. The same woman answered. Her voice was steady, but Dad spoke so quickly that all his words joined together.

'He's-here-the-bear-right-outside-our-cabin-trying-to-get-in!'

'The helicopter will be right there, sir,' she said. 'Stay calm.' Which was very easy for her to say, because she probably didn't have a wild bear trying to smash through a wall to get at her.

Another thud – even louder than the first – and another tremor. I squealed. Zeb too. We were in the furthest corner, staring at the wall. All the furniture was wedged up against the door, but this bear wasn't trying to come in through the door. And now, if he did get in, our only escape route was blocked by a pile of furniture. I shivered with dread. Oates was barking his head off.

Then another thud, and this time the wood splintered

and a large paw crashed through. This time we all squealed.

I glimpsed him through the jagged hole that he'd made – standing on his hind legs, enormous. Ferocious. Dark brown, ragged fur. He was staring at us.

Dad had grabbed the poker, Hunter was gripping the shovel, and they both stood in front of us, ready for action. Zeb had taken a branch from beside the fire, and was swishing it like a sword. But I remembered what the survival book had said, and picked up the two empty metal mugs and was clattering them together and yelling, to make as much noise as I could.

'Good plan!' yelled Dad. 'Everyone, make some noise!'

Hunter started roaring. Zeb was whooping. I was yelling and clanking the mugs. Dad, in his opera voice, was booming 'Go away, bear!' over and over.

The bear stared at us a moment longer, then threw his head back and roared – an utterly terrifying sight – and then he crashed down onto all fours.

The noise seemed to be working, but the bear wasn't slinking away. He stayed where he was, just outside the cabin.

Then the helicopter got louder, lower. The searchlight was dazzling. That's when it happened – they shot him with a dart.

Barney stumbled, hit the muddy ground and then lay there, perfectly still. Nobody moved for a while. We looked at each other, wide-eyed, still not daring to speak, and then we all stepped forward to peer through the hole in the wall. The bear was lying there, face down, with a tranquilliser dart sticking out of his enormous hairy bum.

The gust from the helicopter as it touched down ruffled our hair and the fur of the sleeping bear too. Then the blades slowed with a loud groan and – eventually – stopped. After all the noise and all the action, everything was calm and quiet.

The crew piled out of the helicopter: two men and a woman, all wearing dark green uniforms with orange fluoro bibs. One man was the pilot, and the other man and the woman both had tranquilliser rifles, which they were still pointing at the bear in case it moved. The woman asked us, in a loud voice, if we were all right. We shouted, 'Yes,' and then she told us to stay where we were for the moment.

When they were completely sure that Barney was in a deep, deep sleep, the woman shouted that it was okay for us to come out of the cabin. We dragged the furniture away from the door and went outside. Oates was normally really curious about any new animal. He either barked at them or sniffed them or, usually, both. But one look at Barney close up, and he whimpered and cowered behind Dad. He was smart after all.

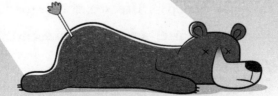

The woman walked over to us and said that her name was Claire.

'Are you all okay?' she asked. 'No one's hurt?'

We were still a bit stunned and out of breath – being charged by a furry killing-machine will do that to you – but Dad said, 'We're fine, I think.' He nodded at the hole in the wall. 'We've got a brand-new window,' he said, as if that was a good thing, 'and it might take a while for our pulses to return to normal. But, other than that – we're pretty good.' He looked around to see if we agreed. We all nodded.

But Claire went to the helicopter anyway, came back with a first-aid bag and did some tests on us.

'I need to check you over,' she said. 'You've all had a nasty fright.'

She checked my pulse and my breathing, and put this tight bit of material around my upper arm and pumped it up to test my blood pressure. Then she looked into my eyes, to check my pupils. After me, she checked Zeb, Dad and Hunter and, after a few more questions, she was happy that we were all basically okay.

'We can evacuate you, if you like,' she said. 'Get you

out of here in the helicopter. Though we'll have to give Barney a lift home first, before he wakes up. He seems pretty grumpy at the best of times. I wouldn't like to see him when he's just woken.'

Dad and Hunter looked at me and Zeb, to see what we wanted to do. I was pretty tempted by the thought of a night-time helicopter ride – it sounded extremely cool. But I was also completely exhausted, and I'd had more than enough excitement for one day. Zeb seemed to be feeling the same way.

'I'm happy to stay,' he said with a shrug.

'As long as there are no other escaped animals,' I said. 'A tiger on the loose, for instance. Or a rampaging rhino.'

Claire smiled.

'They've counted all the animals at the safari park, twice, to make sure. They'd moved Barney to a holding pen while they were doing renovations to his enclosure, but the fence obviously wasn't high enough for him. They've assured us it's just the one bear.'

We all looked at Barney, who didn't seem like 'just' anything, sprawled on the muddy ground in front of us. He was completely enormous. No wonder Hunter had clambered up the tree when he'd seen him. While Claire was making sure we were all okay, the two men laid out a massive net on the ground. Then all three of them – Claire too – tried to roll the bear onto it. They strained and groaned, but they couldn't manage it. So we all helped. His fur was warm, and he smelled really bad. Now that I'd been up close to a grizzly bear, I would never complain about Ernest's nappies again.

Barney was incredibly heavy, like a huge hairy boulder. But eventually, with a lot of effort and loads of grunting, we managed to roll him onto his back, onto the net. Seeing his face again was terrifying. but once I'd got over the shock, he didn't look nearly so dangerous.

The crew tied the net up with metal clips, before bringing out a massive thick rope and attaching one end to the net and the other end to the helicopter.

Barney looked surprisingly peaceful in there, like he was in a huge hammock, just having a doze.

I wondered if bears had dreams and, if they did, I wondered what he was dreaming about right now.

After checking that the net was safe, Claire strode over to us.

'Thanks for your help,' she said. 'You were all incredibly brave.' Then to me she added, 'I've got a girl your age at home, Holly. Her name's Wren. I can't wait to tell her that I just shot a bear. In the bum.'

I laughed, but then I suddenly remembered my own mum – and I was guessing that the escaped bear would be all over the news. If Mum was watching it on TV, she'd be completely sick with worry. I said this to Dad – he gasped, agreed and, after checking with Hunter that it was okay to use his phone, he handed it to me. I dialled.

'Hello?' said Mum. It was completely brilliant to hear her voice.

'Hi, Mum.'

'Holly?'

'Yes.'

'What's happening? That wouldn't be a screen that you're using to call me, would it?'

'No. Yes. I mean – have you been watching the news?'

'No – Ernest and I are having a mostly screen-free time ourselves. Although we did watch that renovations show last night – you know, the one that you don't like. Your brother absolutely insisted on watching it.'

'I bet.'

'Wait – have *you* been watching the news? How? What's going on? Have you left the cabin? Is something wrong? How did you get a phone? What's happening? Where are you?'

That was a crazy amount of questions, even for Mum,

so I just said, 'Look, we're completely fine, and don't go nuts, but – there was a bear. On the loose. In the woods.'

'Ha. Good one,' she said. 'Hilarious. Did Dad put you up to this?'

'I'm serious, Mum. It tried to get into the cabin just now.'

'Of course it did. Did it huff? Did it puff? Did it blow the cabin down? No, wait – that was the big, bad wolf, wasn't it? What was it that the three bears did again?'

'Turn the TV on, Mum. I bet it's on there right now.'

She was quiet for a few seconds while she found the remote and clicked on the news channel. And then:

'Oh. My. Goodness. Are you okay, my little sausage?'

'I'm good,' I told her. What was it with my parents and sausages?

'What about Dad and Oates?'

'They're both completely fine. The emergency people came and tranquillised Barney.'

'Barney?'

'The bear. It was amazing. Like something out of a movie. And now they're about to take him away.'

'Good grief! Is Dad there? Can you put him on?'

I did. They talked for a few seconds, and then Dad said he had to go, so that Zeb could call *his* mum.

Zeb's mum, unfortunately, *had* been watching the news, and had been worried out of her mind. Zeb's sisters, too, had been sitting there on the sofa in stunned silence (which was an all-time first, according to Zeb). He tried to calm his mum down, but eventually gave up and passed the phone to his dad, who wasn't a whole lot more successful in getting a word in.

Hunter seemed to have recovered from the whole bear thing, but he turned pale again as he tried to tell Zeb's mum that everything was okay. I actually felt really sorry for him. In one night he'd faced a grizzly bear and then had to face Zeb's mum, who sounded almost as terrifying. It must have been his worst nightmare.

Soon the emergency crew had finished up, and we thanked them. Loads. Hunter shook their hands so strongly that I thought their arms would come off.

They said goodbye, got into the helicopter and took off, really carefully. It was an incredible sight, the helicopter flying off towards the safari park, with Barney dangling in the net below, high above the trees.

I'd always wanted to be an explorer, like Dad. Then, after the Dadventure, I'd wondered about becoming an archaeologist, like Mum. But now I saw that being a helicopter-based rescue-person like Claire would be a pretty incredible job too. Working as part of a well-trained emergency team – it seemed brilliant.

I'd always thought of adventures as something you have on your own, but now I could see how cool it was to work with others. And it wasn't just Claire and the two helicopter guys that had shown me that. It was us too: Zeb and I had found his dad, and discovered the bear poo and bear tracks. Oates had found my dad. Dad had talked Hunter down from the tree. And then Hunter had got us back safely, and rescued the phone. All of us had played a part.

When the helicopter had gone, everything went quiet again, and dark.

We invited Zeb and his dad to stay the night with us in the cabin, and they were happy to accept. Hunter fetched their sleeping bags, mats and pillows, and then laid them on our floor, by the fireplace.

I was completely shattered by now – my pocket watch

said it was nearly one in the morning! – but my brain was still super-active from all the terror and excitement, and it seemed like the others were feeling the same way. Except Oates, that is – he was already asleep by the fire, snoring his head off. Dogs are really lucky like that.

Dad and Hunter were sitting at the table, talking in low voices about the bear, and then they moved on to grown-up subjects like work and families and cars. Zeb and I, meanwhile, were talking about much more interesting things: movies, games, music, books, and also about stuff that we'd done. I told him about the Dadventure.

And it might seem an incredibly strange thing to say about the day that we almost got eaten by a bear, but – it was one of the absolute best days of my life.

15 Triple Task Thursday

When I woke up, light was streaming in through the new hole in the wall. I groped under my pillow until I felt the cold metal of the pocket watch, then I squinted at the time as I wound it – it was 10 a.m. already. Oates and Zeb were still asleep, snuggled up in front of the fire and looking pretty cute. Hunter's sleeping bag was empty, and when I groggily climbed out of my bunk and looked up at Dad's bed, I saw that *he'd* gone out too: two missing dads! *Not again*, I thought. But when I opened the door, there was Dad, sitting on the front step, with the pad of paper in his lap and a pen in his hand.

'Morning,' he said.

'What are you doing?' I asked sleepily.

'Writing up last night's story,' he said.

'Boothby Bennett?' I said. Dad's bedtime story seemed like days ago already – weeks.

'No,' he said, grinning. 'Not Boothby Bennett – *our* story, the bear.'

I narrowed my eyes. 'Can you please leave me out of it this time?'

'Don't be daft,' he said. 'You're the absolute heroes, you and Zeb. Tracking down the dads. Identifying the bear poo and the bear prints. Being brave. Making a noise to keep it at bay. And I'll make extra-sure that I don't embarrass you this time – you can even check it before I send it off, if you like. It's called "copy approval".'

I sighed, and looked around.

'Where's Hunter?'

Dad shrugged.

'He must have gone for a walk,' he said, then added, mischievously, 'I wonder what he'll bump into this time.'

Oates woke Zeb up by licking his face. There must be worse ways of being woken, but I can't think of many.

They both came outside, Zeb sleepy, Oates bounding with energy. Zeb asked me where his dad was, and I could only shrug. But a few minutes later, we heard a very loud 'Ahoy!'

Hunter strode out of the trees towards us. In one hand he was holding a fishing rod. In the other was a net containing two freshly caught, medium-sized fish.

'I dropped my fishing things last night, when I met Barney,' he said, in a big, confident voice. 'So I went back to get them, and it's a lot easier to catch fish first thing in the morning – especially now there are no bears around.' He flashed us a grin. 'We'll cook you a special breakfast to say thanks for last night – and then –' he looked at Zeb apologetically – 'we'll have to go home.'

'But . . .'

'Mum insisted,' Hunter said firmly. 'No discussion.'

Hunter hurried off to the tent to get some ingredients and cooking equipment, and Zeb reluctantly followed him.

I felt sorry for Zeb. The old Hunter seemed to be back, the super-confident one, and I think I liked him more last night, when he was scared.

'We should probably be going home too,' Dad said to me.

'Do we have to?'

'I thought you'd want to go back. You certainly wanted to yesterday – and that was *before* we'd met Barney.'

I sighed. 'Well, it would be nice see Mum and Ernest again,' I said, 'and sleep in my own bed, in a room without a bear hole in the wall. But there's only one day left, isn't there?'

'And you'd like to finish the Mumbelievable Challenge, I suppose?'

I nodded.

I had to admit – the whole 'challenge' thing didn't seem quite so important now. Not since we'd had an actual life-or-death adventure, but it still didn't feel right to give up when we were so close to the end – plus there was Mum's mystery prize to think of too. I went into the cabin and came straight back out again clutching the light green envelope with 'Thursday' written on it. I tore it open and read the note inside.

Hi, Holly

Only one more sleep to go

before I see you again. I can't wait!

Today is Triple Task Thursday!

Your tasks are:

Teach Dad something.

Get Dad to teach you something. And . . .

Have an exciting nature adventure with Dad.

Love you!

Mum

I smiled and passed the note to Dad.

I knew exactly what Mum was trying to do. She'd been worried that Dad and I wouldn't be getting on, because of the whole newspaper-article thing, and so she had set a challenge that would make us work together. But what she couldn't have known, of course, when she'd come up with the task, was that we'd already done this, and done it spectacularly.

'Well, we can tick off task three, can't we?' said Dad. 'Because it was after midnight when Barney had a snooze – so it was technically "today". And "nature adventures" don't get much more exciting than an encounter with a huge bear, do they?'

'True.'

'And, now that I think about it,' he added, 'you've already taught me something today too.'

'I have?'

'Yes – that you're incredibly brave, Holly, and resourceful, and grown up.'

I smiled, but then I shook my head.

'It would feel a bit like cheating though. Because the brave bit was definitely yesterday. After midnight, when

162

Barney was trying to smash down the wall, I was mostly just screaming my head off.'

Dad giggled.

'That makes two of us then,' he said. 'In that case, you need to think of something else to teach me. And I'll try to think of what I can teach you. Though I'm not sure that I can any more,' he added very proudly. 'Not when you already know the sausage song.'

About half an hour later, Zeb and Hunter came back to the cabin with a plate of filleted fish, some freshly picked mushrooms and herbs, some cooking stuff and a sheet of tarpaulin.

Zeb built up our fire, boiled some water and added things to the pot – rice, chunks of fish, the mushrooms and herbs, salt and pepper. He really seemed to be enjoying himself, like a chef on TV. His dad, meanwhile, was cutting up the tarpaulin and using a piece of it to patch up the hole in the wall, holding it in place with nails from the smashed-up pieces of wood and using a flat stone as a hammer to drive the nails in. Dad was crouching next to him trying to help, but was mostly just getting in the way.

Breakfast – when Zeb ladled it out into our bowls – was a sloppy, fishy, ricey, mushroomy porridge, which sounds completely horrible, I know, and it looked horrible too, like something you might get to eat in prison, and not a nice prison either. But Zeb explained that it was called a 'congee', and that Chinese people have it for breakfast a lot.

'One billion people can't be wrong,' Dad told him, and blew on his portion to cool it.

I sat on the floor with the others and frowned at the porridge. But then I remembered how I'd been with calamari and tofu on the Dadventure. I'd pulled a face then too, but they'd ended up tasting really nice. Besides, I was completely starving by now. And so – grimacing – with the bowl warming my lap, I tried a spoonful. It took me a few moments to make up my mind – but it was honestly brilliant, like a delicious thick soup. It warmed me up inside and filled me up too. This porridge was just right. I nodded at Zeb. He was totally brilliant at cooking.

When we'd finished, Dad and I washed up, and Zeb and his dad went off to pack up their tent. Then it was time for them to go. They came back over to us, with their huge backpacks on. I was feeling happy-sad: sad that Zeb was going, but happy that I'd met him. We'd swapped email addresses, so we could keep in touch, but it wouldn't be the same.

Hunter shook our hands – very firmly, real bone-crunchers, and thanked us. It was hard to be sure, but it seemed like last night had changed him, at least a bit.

I really hoped so. Having a dad like mine who is forever making jokes can be a bit tiring. But having a dad who is always making you feel small, that would be completely horrible. At least Hunter seemed to be a bit kinder now. He'd even said nice things about Zeb's cooking this morning.

Zeb shook our hands too – a lot more gently than his dad had done – and said goodbye.

'Good luck,' I said, and we watched them walk off into the woods.

It was really quiet when they'd gone.

Dad did some more writing at the table, and I sat on my bunk, reading my book. I was getting to a really exciting bit near the end, and I wanted to finish it, but there was another part of me that didn't want to, because then I'd be saying goodbye to the characters until their next adventure – which was waiting for me in my room at home, but that was an entire day away.

In the end though, I just couldn't help myself. I raced through the last few pages: then I sighed and closed the book, happy-sad again.

Dad looked up from his writing.

'Good book, was it?' he asked. I nodded, and then he stood up, went over to his rucksack, dug deep to the bottom of it and pulled out . . . a book. And not just any book either, but the next one in the series: the one that I'd thought was back in my room at home.

I whooped. Then I actually hugged him. It took him by surprise. He hugged me back, a really squeezy one, and it took me a few seconds to wriggle out of it.

'So,' he said, 'have you thought about what you're going to teach me?'

'How about "How to use a compass"?' I said. 'Or "How not to get lost in the woods"?'

'Ha. Hilarious.'

'Or what about "How not to embarrass me in front of boys"?'

'That might actually be useful,' he said. 'I'm listening. How can I do that?'

'Let me see: a) keep your clothes on – and, b) don't talk. Ever. And definitely don't sing songs about meat products.'

'Got it.' He tapped his head, to show that this advice was now safely stored inside his brain. 'Actually,' he

said, 'I was really hoping that you'd show me how to make an origami boat.'

So I did – at the table, with his 'I-pad'. Dad was a really slow learner. His first attempt was all wonky. The second looked more like a hat than a boat. But the third one was actually okay. He looked really proud of himself.

'Now,' he said, 'it's my turn to teach *you* something, and I know just what: it's something that might have come in handy last night in fact.'

He put the index and middle fingers of both hands into the corners of his mouth, and whistled. Really loudly. It almost burst my eardrums.

Oates went completely crazy.

'I can barely do a normal whistle,' I said, when my ears had stopped ringing. 'I'll never be able to do *that*.'

'With that attitude,' said Dad, 'you're absolutely right. But if you put your mind to it, I bet you'll be able to do it before the end of the day.'

And – unbelievably – he was right. It took a lot of time. And coaching. And persistence. And practice. Plus a whole lot of dribble. But by sunset I could whistle, really loud. The only problem was that, when I'd eventually got the hang of it, I wouldn't stop, and Dad was regretting that he'd ever taught me.

16 Hero

I was supposed to be the magician in the family, but Dad was full of surprises too. Instead of using a top hat though, he kept pulling brilliant things out of his rucksack.

My book had been a fantastic enough surprise (I was already up to page seventy-nine). But then, after dinner on our last night in the cabin (canned chicken soup), as the light was starting to fade, he delved right to the bottom of his bag and produced a squashed but completely delicious pack of marshmallows. We toasted them on twigs over the fire and they were amazing – sticky, warm and gooey. By the end I felt a bit sick, but it was definitely worth it.

And then I had the best night's sleep ever. People say, 'I slept like a baby,' to mean that they had a really good sleep, but I'm not sure that those people have ever lived with a baby, because babies tend to wake up a lot in the night and cry really, really loudly, for ages. Those people should really say, 'I slept like a dog,' instead, because dogs seem to be completely brilliant sleepers. Our dog is, anyway.

When I woke up in the morning, Oates was still dozing, but I practically jumped out of bed. I'd been really looking forward to today, for two reasons. Number one, we'd be seeing Mum and Ernest again and going back home to spend time with our old friend electricity. And, number two, Friday's envelope was the most intriguing one of all. It was purple, and bursting with something inside: something hard in a crinkly wrapper. Something plastic? I'd been wondering about it all week.

I tore open the envelope. There was a note, and the shiny silver wrapper said that the plastic thing was a 'disposable camera'.

'What *is* that exactly?' I asked Dad.

'A long time ago,' he said, 'in olden times, when I

was a boy,

phones were things that were

connected to the wall of your house – you definitely couldn't fit them in your pocket, unless you had completely massive pockets. And we had these amazing things called "cameras".'

I rolled my eyes. 'I know what a camera is, Dad.'

'Well, this is a special kind of camera that you use only once. The film's already inside it, and you get the photos developed in a special place, where they print out the pictures for you. And then they throw the camera away.'

It seemed like a whole lot of effort for just a few photos. But I had to admit it also seemed pretty cool – to take a photo and then have to wait a few days before you could see what it looked like.

I read the note.

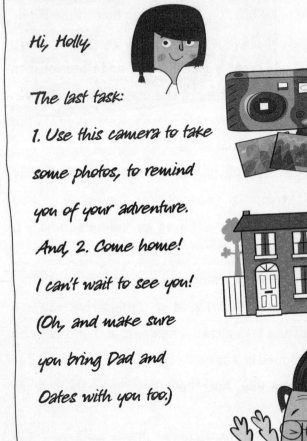

Hi, Holly

The last task:

1. Use this camera to take some photos, to remind you of your adventure. And, 2. Come home! I can't wait to see you! (Oh, and make sure you bring Dad and Oates with you too.)

Lots of love,
Mum (and Ernest) x

So, while Dad packed up our stuff and tidied the cabin, I went around taking photos of everything: trees, the dreaded treasure box, the patched-up hole in the cabin, the imprint that Barney had made in the ground when he'd fallen. Then I took a photo of Dad and Oates next to the fireplace, and a picture of the bunk beds too. It was hard to take a selfie with this camera, so I asked Dad to take a photo of me leaning against the cabin, like I was an experienced explorer.

And then it was time to go, to walk through the woods to the car park where Mum and Ernest would be waiting for us.

I led the way.

The most surprising thing about the Mumbelievable Challenge – apart from meeting Barney of course – was that Dad and I didn't go completely screen-crazy for the second week of the holiday.

Dad had to catch up on his work emails and spent a few hours writing up the story of our dramatic holiday for the newspaper but, other than that, his laptop mostly stayed closed.

I watched a bit of telly and a couple of online origami tutorials, and then I emailed Zeb, but Jumping Guy's adventures didn't seem nearly so exciting any more – not when you'd been face to face with a grizzly bear.

When Mum suggested that we have a family screen-free day every week from now on, Dad and I were actually happy to agree. We chose Sunday, because it was a good day for having adventures. Also, there was never much on telly then. Ernest didn't really understand what was going on, but we knew he'd be completely fine with it too, because it meant that he'd get even more attention than usual. Attention was Ernest's number-one thing in the entire world.

In the second week of the holiday, Dad spent a lot of time going out for walks with Ernest and Oates – all the boys together. Meanwhile, Mum and I did fun stuff, just the two of us: we watched an action movie, went to the science museum, went swimming. And best of all was Mum's prize for finishing the challenge. Two prizes, actually. The first was that I could keep the pocket watch: she said that her grandma would have wanted me to have it – that I was carrying on the long line of adventurous women in her family. Her grandma, she added, was also called Holly, and that was the reason they'd given me that name – so I *was* named after an explorer after all, and not just a prickly plant!

When Mum told me the other prize, I burst out laughing – she'd arranged to take the whole family to the safari park (except Oates of course – no outside animals were allowed).

The safari park is really cool. We had the best day

ever. As well as the animal bit, there's a small theme-park there too and, because the manager was feeling guilty about the bear incident, we got free tickets and unlimited goes on all the rides.

I went on the roller coaster with Dad three times, and we screamed our heads off the whole way, every time.

Roller coasters were one of the many things that Dad was scared of but – as he'd been saying a lot recently – it's good to face your fears. Ernest was too small for all the rides except the Happy Smiley Train, which went around only slightly faster than someone could walk. He seemed to completely love it though. I went on with him twice, and both times he was gurgling with pleasure from start to finish. 'Your brother's an adrenaline-junkie, too,' said Dad.

It wasn't Disneyland, not at all, but it was loads of fun. Mum bought me a candyfloss which was bigger than my head. It was even bigger than Emily Fellows's head, which is really saying something. And then we all got in the car and went to the safari-park bit, which was completely brilliant too.

After we'd driven around most of it – and had camels trying to poke their heads into our car and monkeys trying to snap off our windscreen wipers – we finally saw Barney. I was the first to spot him. He was in the American Zone and, as Mum drove closer, I was very relieved to see that he was safely behind a really high fence. I had to admit, he looked much, much nicer from behind a massive fence. But I waved at him as we drove past anyway, wondering if he remembered us. I wouldn't be forgetting him in a hurry, that was for sure.

On the first day back at school, I was feeling a bit wobbly. So much had happened to me in the two weeks since I'd been there, but I was guessing that nobody would have forgotten about my hotel nudie-run. Kids don't forget things like that. So I was preparing myself for the usual giggling, name-calling and teasing.

Emily Fellows seemed to have other things on her mind though – or at least she did first thing in the morning. She swaggered into class with a Minnie Mouse backpack and was soon describing, to anyone who would listen, pretty much every single thing that she'd done, seen and eaten in Disneyland, as well as every character that she'd met.

I sat in my usual seat next to Asha, and we hardly had time to say hello before Ms Devenport took the register and started the lesson.

'Welcome back, everyone,' she said. 'Good morning, class.'

'Good morning, miss.'

'Now, before we do anything today, there is someone in this class who did something extraordinary in the holidays. And we're hopefully going to find out all about it right now.'

Emily beamed, cleared her throat and was about to start talking, when Ms Devenport held up a copy of a newspaper – the one my dad writes for – and opened it to page five.

Daily News

GRIZZLY SCARE

HOW MY AMAZING DAUGHTER SAVED ME FROM A BEAR

BY JAMES CHAMBERS

Everyone was suddenly looking at me. I blushed. Felt sick.

But then I noticed something – no one was smirking. Of course Emily Fellows was looking pretty cranky. But everyone else seemed really interested.

Asha nudged me. 'You're famous again,' she whispered, beaming. 'But in a good way this time.'

'So, Holly,' said Ms Devenport, 'can you tell us what happened?'

'You wrestled a bear?' said Harrison Duffy admiringly.

Everyone laughed.

'Not wrestled,' I said. 'But it did try to smash its way into our cabin – while we were inside.'

There were gasps.

Everyone was listening open-mouthed. You could have heard a paperclip drop.

I felt absolutely amazing – like I was a famous explorer who'd come triumphantly home and now everyone wanted to hear about my adventures. Like a hero who'd risked her life and lived to tell the tale.

So I started from the beginning.

'My mum challenged me and Dad to survive for five

nights in a log cabin, in the middle of a forest, with no electricity . . .'

There were already some gasps.

I couldn't wait to see their faces when I got to the face-off with the bear.

THE END

The Sausage Song

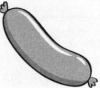

(1st verse)

I had a sausage

A lovely little sausage

And I put it in the oven for my tea.

I went down to the cellar

To fetch my um-ber-ella

And the sausage came after me.

(2nd verse)

That little sausage

That lovely little sausage

That came into the cellar after me.

It bounced up and down

And then went into town

So all I had was chips and peas.

Dave Lowe grew up in Dudley in the West Midlands, and now lives in Brisbane, Australia, with his wife and two daughters. He spends his days writing books, drinking lots of tea, and treading on Lego that his daughters have left lying around. Dave's Stinky and Jinks books follow the adventures of a nine-year-old boy called Ben, and Stinky, Ben's genius pet hamster. (When Dave was younger, he had a pet hamster too. Unlike Stinky, however, Dave's hamster didn't often help him with his homework.) Find Dave online at @daveloweauthor or www.davelowebooks.com

Born in York in the late 1970s, **The Boy Fitz Hammond** now lives in Edinburgh with his wife and their two sons. A freelance illustrator for well over a decade, he loves to draw in a variety of styles, allowing him to work on a range of projects across all media. Find him online at www.nbillustration.co.uk/the-boy-fitz-hammond or on Twitter @tbfhDotCom

Piccadilly

P R E S S

Thank you for choosing a Piccadilly Press book.

If you would like to know more about our authors, our books or if you'd just like to know what we're up to, you can find us online.

www.piccadillypress.co.uk

You can also find us on:

We hope to see you soon!